JOHN F. DEANE was born on Achill I
Dublin where he edits the Dedalus Pi
Ireland, the national poetry society, a.__ ..._ journal *Poetry Ireland Review*. He has published several collections of poetry, the most recent being *Walking on Water* (1994) and *Christ, with Urban Fox* (1997). A collection of his work in French translation (*L'ombre du photographe*) has been published in Lyon and another (*Christ, avec renard urbain*) appeared in Luxembourg in 1998 with drawings by Tony O'Malley. His first collection of short stories, *Free Range*, was published by Wolfhound Press (1994). His novels, *One Man's Place* (1994) and *Flightlines* (1995) were published by Poolbeg. He was awarded the O'Shaughnessy Prize for Poetry in 1998, from the Center for Irish Studies, St Paul, Minnesota. His third novel, *In the Name of the Wolf*, was published by Blackstaff Press in 1999.

The Coffin Master
and other stories

JOHN F. DEANE

THE
BLACKSTAFF
PRESS
BELFAST

First published in 2000 by
The Blackstaff Press Limited
Blackstaff House, Wildflower Way, Apollo Road
Belfast BT12 6TA, Northern Ireland
with the assistance of
The Arts Council of Northern Ireland

ARTS
COUNCIL
of Northern Ireland

Typeset by Techniset Typesetters, Newton-le-Willows, Merseyside

Printed in Ireland by ColourBooks Limited

A CIP catalogue record for this book
is available from the British Library

ISBN 0-85640-664-3

ACKNOWLEDGEMENTS

Some of these stories have been published in the *Honest Ulsterman*, the *Big Spoon*, *Nocturnal Submissions* (Australia), *Phoenix 1*, *Raconteur*, have been broadcast on RTÉ Radio 1, and have won prizes in the Francis MacManus Award, *Raconteur*, the Maurice Walsh Competition, and received the Special Award of the Irish Congress of Trade Unions.

CONTENTS

RITUALS OF DEPARTURE

There was a cavern, moist and echoing, far down inside his brain. Someone was at work in there, drilling. The skull bone juddered under the relentless, erratic pressure. Down through the shuddering of his jaws, his whole body, making it shiver with the cold of extreme pain. He was too old for this, too frail. He should split apart, like an antique delft jug falling back into dust. If he closed his eyes, only scarlet and cobalt flames danced behind the lids. If he opened them the light from outside came against him with a violent intensity.

Everything passes, he said to himself. Everything, even pain.

All life death does end and each day dies with sleep.

He was alone. Perhaps, in the afternoon, the nurse would call. Would find him. Lift his stone-heavy head against her breast and hold a glass of water to his mouth. Drop two tiny white angels onto his burning tongue. It would be a cool breeze moving over the meadow of his fever, bringing stillness, silence, peace. He longed for that relief. He screamed for it with a drawn-out, soundless scream. And he knew he would refuse it, should she come.

He could telephone if things became wholly unbearable. He could almost reach the telephone from where he lay. Just an extra heave of his body in the bed. The soft piano touch of his fingers on the numbers. But he doubted if he could get his body to respond to the brain's commands. That dreadful nausea was not only in his stomach but seemed to fill his entire body. Should he move it was likely his whole being would void itself in total distress. He could wait for those few moments when all the pain halted within him, when all the agony and bitterness withdrew for a while. Like a wave. Then he could move. And call. But he knew that he would not move. Nor call. And if he had the strength he would pull the phonecord from the wall and shove home the bolts on the front door.

The room around him seemed to buzz with the presence of its furnishings. On the walls the old, plum red paper of another century. The great oak wardrobe that was so heavy it seemed to have grown downwards into the floor. The chair, high-backed, upholstered, the pockmarks of woodworm holes, varnished over and over again. As if objects could exist for always, content to stand in the aura of their own silence. He had folded his clothes, as perfectly as always, and laid them over that chair. Last night. A lifetime ago. Last night. There were cobwebs in the high corners of the room. Perhaps the tiny husks of lives whose vital fluids had been sucked out a long time ago. All hanging there in silence. Unpurified, since she had gone. The floorboards polished and trodden for generations, the chinks between them imperceptibly soldering each to each with the minuscule shedding of human flesh and the silent decaying of the bodies of creeping things. The doorknob, its roundness worn by years upon years of handling, how it hung a little askew, a little loose, brown and matt and indifferent. It should all go up into the purity of flames.

He was so old now, so light, he had not known there would be so much flesh and bone left to suffer. He was so old that, when he walked out at evening, the people scarcely seemed to notice him, as if he were a statue in an overgrown niche to whom devotion had petered out years ago. So old, the children did not reckon him. So old that only his youth came clearly to him now. As if, coming almost full circle in his life, the gauze that separated his last moments from his earliest had grown wafer thin, delicate as the host held high against summer light.

He had dealt unkindly with Lizzie then. With Janet, too. Leaving a great stain on his life, an ugly fault. Almost a month before their marriage, when he strutted like a red stag among his peers, Lizzie Curley had fallen at his feet. Certain then of his life's future, he had stolen away that August afternoon, riding his bike down the dirt track to the cove. The sea was mute and cowed in that rocky haven, low cliffs rising and gleaming under the warm sun. The narrow bed of sand was dry as cotton under a canopy of rock.

Lizzie was wearing a light blue dress with white buttons all the way from neck to hem. Her face was pale and pretty. Her hair, rust-coloured with little flashes of sunset gold, moved with a lilting rhythm around her face. Her eyes, deep and kindly and of a blue so gentle they stirred his being towards remorse, held a longing, appealing cry to him. But she was so simple, God help her, so simple and trusting she could be of no use to him in his life. She moved her body in an unconscious rhythm of loss then, and he, supreme and *bienfaisant*, took the great gift she offered him and gave her nothing in return. Till he left her, waving back a kiss into the darkening cove, turning towards the house of his betrothed. Poor, foolish Lizzie, all douceur and dullness, had left the island and he had never heard of her again.

His wife had not known about Lizzie, but sometimes, when he and Janet lay breast upon breast, lips upon lips, Lizzie

Curley's soft cries of pleasure and loss echoed in his brain and something fell away from the perfect love he imagined to be his and Janet's.

He knew now that the cocksure sprightliness of spring is coloured bitter lemon, that the maturing of the fall and early winter is a dark green that is heavy-hearted, fruited with regrets. There were all those miserable crimes, infractions of the petty laws, the little trespasses and sad transgressions that add their cumulative stain to the soul. He remembered them now, they flickered across the bleary, unfocused screen of his memory as they went hurrying past.

The nurse had called when pain like this had first stricken him. He had been in bed then, too, irritable and directionless. She had soothed and scolded him, settling his body into a comforting coolness, injecting something into his arm that was a blessed dullness rapidly travelling through his body, distributing insensitivity and sweet oblivion. A clogging impurity that left him withering, but without pain. Should she come now with her morphine, he must refuse, he must avoid insensitivity and oblivion, he had to see his life through.

It ought to have been – magnificent! with Janet. How is it that two who love each other so much can hurt each other so often? as if the stain on his life had tarnished everything he touched. And then, when Janet died, when he stood, perplexed and bowed and grieving over that hole that was to swallow her up, how he had rebelled, scrabbling over the mound of sodden daub and down through the artificial grass onto her coffin, to see her again, to touch her one last time . . . But even as he scraped at the polished wood, even as hands reached for him and the women sobbed and murmured, horrified, he knew he was but a stained old fool. He let them lift him bodily out of her grave, but he had ripped the small brass crucifix from above her nameplate and held it secretly against his chest.

He stood among them again, breathing quietly, nodding his head in acknowledgement of his sin.

When they tried to usher him away, the last prayers said, her soul commended to the angels that they should conduct her into paradise, he would not move. He waited, and the rain fell, making its own softly grieving sound in the heavy leaves of the trees. The gravediggers shifted restlessly, watching him, but he motioned to them and they began. The earth fell with an ugly thudding sound on her coffin and each bleak fall thumped misery into his heart. The gravediggers, suffering the rain, quickly forgot the broken man standing by the trees, the comforters waiting in the sleek black cars. Until his long, low howl rose suddenly into a scream of anger and despair and he took the crucifix and spat on it like a wild cat spitting out its anger. He took it then and flung it, with all his power, away into the undergrowth beyond the graves, and he fell to his knees. *Pitched past pitch of grief.*

Now, where he lay, the agony scalded his very bones. If he could only die now, only yield to the bliss of insensibility. But the acid pain rose slowly along his body, as if his blood ran sulphur, as if his flesh, muscles, sinews, were steeped in bubbling oil. And he thanked God for it, for his isolation, for the bitterness, for the slow, relentless purification he was forced to undergo.

Exhausted then, he passed from consciousness into some state of being that was not life, not death. And lay, spent. Forgiven. And forgiving.

Sometime in the evening he awoke. A gentle light fell through the window and tiny motes of dust moved through it. He turned his head towards the light. He felt no pain.

'Thank Christ,' he whispered aloud. 'Thank Christ it's over.'

Outside, swallows had begun to gather on the wires, and

sat, restless, waiting. He got out of bed slowly and dressed himself with great care. He came to the door and gazed out over the yellow meadow towards the line of trees on the horizon. The narrow road lay like a stream of still water. Everything was silence. And the fullness before the fall. He took his hat off the hatstand. He chose his favourite walking stick. He put on a light overcoat. He closed the door softly behind him. For a while he stood on the doorstep, watching. Then he settled his old body into its walking shape and set out.

He turned left onto Donnelly's Lane and went down the gentle slope into the valley. He hesitated a moment before turning right onto Sweetman's Road. The sun was a lovely damson colour, hovering over the trees. The sky was stippled with tiny clouds, pink and rose and madder. He pulled the brim of his hat down a fraction to shade his eyes. He began to walk more briskly, then, on the path that rose towards that setting sun, the point of the stick tapping the road with a regular, pleasing rhythm.

He found, as he walked, he was gathering strength and vigour in his limbs. All around him, though it was close to dusk, things had taken on a lovely clarity. He felt he could stride on thus for ever. Up the paths of air. The sun dropped behind the trees, leaving on the sky the warm glow of memory. He walked as a younger man would walk, the top of the hedgerows several feet below him now. As if the surface he walked on were made of the softest mountain moss and he walked upon it with the naked feet of young, pure love. He felt a great catch of joy in his throat. Breathing was easy, the tops of the trees passing below him and he could see down into the forest's darkness where he had never seen before. Should he break out into song, he knew there would be nobody, nobody to pay him heed.

They found his clothes, shoes, underwear, overcoat, all laid out neatly on the road. The way clothes are laid, in preparation for a special evening, out upon a bed. And all the appurtenances a life accumulates in its long pilgrimage, the two gold teeth, the spectacles, the hearing aid, the ring. His hat and stick propped carefully against a fence post, done with, gratified, bequeathed.

THE EXPERIENCE OF WHAT
IS BEAUTIFUL

My name is Bendy. Bendy M'Glynn. My wife's name is Flo. *Was* Flo. Florence. Flo and Bendy we were, Bendy and Flo. Like a gurgling mountain stream. Benedict Christopher M'Glynn was a ton weight on my back. But I was always happy with Bendy. A familiar, yielding twang to it, wouldn't you say?

The flags of the kitchen floor are a mess. I've straightened out poor Flo's skirts. She is lying on the flags. The thick woollen stockings looked ugly just under her knees, the flesh of her thighs showed lumpy and grey. I couldn't leave her like that. Poor Flo. I've given her a modicum of dignity and that's the way I'll always remember her, stretched across the flags of the kitchen floor.

I have always believed in order, constabulary order. That's why I'm writing all of this down. So that you'll know, and all will be in order again, after a fashion. There's not much order about me now, only the slow creep and congeal that blood makes by its own hesitant flowing, finding canals between the stone flags, settling in pool-holes and intimate crevasses of the floor.

What is in order is beautiful and you can see the quiet face of

God in it. On the mantelpiece for instance: two china dogs, big-eyed, pup-handsome, one at either end, watching out into the kitchen; the holy water next, little plastic flasks shaped like the Virgin with her blue gown; photographs, nicely framed: Patsy, Jackie, handsome in their wedding clothes, all of them cared for, placed and remembered. The two brass candlesticks almost in the centre and between them the small statue, the Child Jesus of Prague, red-mantled, the child's face blessed and blessing. Order, God's sacred presence visible through it all.

We kept hens, you see, or maybe you don't see, not yet. Out in the back, behind our little house. There was a fine patch of ground and we fenced it in with stakes and chicken-fencing and a dandy little gate to allow us exit and entrance. A tongue-and-groove house with flaps and perches. An enclosure. A perfect parallelogram. Rich in grit and pebbles. Ground oyster shells. And light, lots of lovely light.

'You see here,' I used to say to Flo, 'the universe in miniature. Night to follow day, eggs from hens and hens from eggs, an orderly, predictable procession of events. The essence of happiness and peace.'

'And the killing?' she asked, a quiet humour in her old, sly eyes. I didn't choose to respond to that question. Not then, anyway. First I had to learn about bumblefoot, arthritis, blepharitis, crazy chick disease, rickets, worms... We were standing by the fence gate when she said that, so quickly old, alone together after all the years of rearing and caring. Alone with our hens and cockerels, our little house that had fallen silent again, the way a babbling river drops into a dark, still pool, alone with our evenings, Bendy and Flo clucking contentedly together. The twilight content of God in our lives.

Today, it all collapsed at my feet. It was late afternoon, early evening. Poor Flo had just boiled our eggs for supper. Have you known the delicious goodness of an egg lightly boiled, spooned into a cup with a scoop of butter, a pinch of salt and a dusting of pepper, stirred and stirred, eaten with white bread toasted? We were getting ready to sit together by the fire. Soon it would be news time on TV, we would have finished the eggs and be set to enjoy a fine cup of tea. Where we live you can hear a vehicle coming down the long lane. Flo peeked out the kitchen window, just a peek from between the bitter-apple curtains.

''Tis a blue van,' she said. 'An old blue van. There's dunts on it. It's a strange one. I can't see who's within.'

They had shut off the engine. There came a silence then; I don't know how it was but I sensed a menace in that silence and in the strangeness of this visitation. She and I, God rest and bless her, had lived so long in the order of our security that we were subtle beings, buoyed on instinct. Fear was not a thing we knew too well. Perhaps it would have been better if we had learned how to fear, or had never forgotten what fear is. I heard the van doors open and shut loudly. I heard footsteps across the gravel. I did not fret. But poor Flo sat down heavily on her old chair at the fireplace and I could see the greyness that had taken over her face; I could hear an old clanking sound of dread coming from her. Her eyes fixed on the kitchen door.

We woke up one night, I remember, oh a few years gone, to hear a fierce commotion from the hen run. Cluckings and flurries and demented squawks. Flo sat up in bed in the darkness. I couldn't see her but I knew she put her two hands to her head.

'Armageddon!' she said. She had a fine sense of humour, poor Flo.

I got up that night, put on my slippers and dressing gown, switched on the light over the back door and flung the door open at one and the same instant. I knew it: a great flurry of feathers under the cold white light from the bulb and there, startled so that he and I looked for one long second into each other's eyes – a fox! beautiful, a perfect form of sleek and orange-red, his lush tail tipped with white; a hen dangling from his mouth. In the glance we exchanged there was a moment of understanding and respect, an acknowledgement of one another's rights.

'You'll have to get a shotgun,' Flo whispered from behind my shoulder. By the time I looked back from her, fox and hen had disappeared. I shook my head.

'No gun,' I said. 'No gun. Never.'

Next day I went all around my fencing. I had thought it perfect, I had dug it down into the earth so that a fox could not squeeze in underneath it. I had thought it sound, mathematically capped, fitted and laid out. But he had found a spot of softer earth, he had dug, he had defeated me, and I laughed with appreciation of his skill.

When the loud knock came to the door I thought of that night, Flo's whispered 'Armageddon', and the word 'shotgun' came floating into my head. How quickly the mind can slip out of its ordered path, how easily and willingly it will yield from what is necessary to what is chaotic. I got up and went to the door.

There were two of them, big men, not old, not young. Ugly.

'Got any ol' scrap, mister?' the first one said, quickly and aggressively. The second one was already edging himself into the doorway; he was looking beyond me, into the house. Practised eyes, a grin already formed about his mouth.

'I don't think . . .' I began, but he interrupted me.

'Any ol' pots or irons or furniture even, or maybe a bit a' brass, or copper, or anythin' at all you could sell?'

All the while the second fellow was pushing himself forward, actually shoving me back into the kitchen. The first one wore a dirty woollen cap, black or navy it was; the second man was bald, no, not bald, but he looked as if his head had been shaven close. The way they scalp the hedgerows nowadays, the young farmers, too eager to make use of every scrap of field, too happy to let the young birdlings die. Woollen cap had a big ring in his left ear, shaven head, a small silver ring in his left nostril. Funny how you notice such things. They were dirty-looking, with dark jackets, baggy trousers, a smell of sweat and rust and urine off them both, their hands big and fidgeting, their nails filthy. Before I knew it they were in the kitchen and the door was closed behind them.

'I'm afraid we have nothing . . .' I tried again.

'Excuse us, missus,' woollen cap said, looking at Flo, a great grin on his face, a black hole in his mouth where several teeth were missing. 'We're only lookin' for a bit a help, like. Some money now, or jewels or such. You know?'

Flo sat frozen before them, her eyes fixed as if she were a hen hypnotised by a fox. Woollen cap pulled out the chair I had been using near Flo and he sat himself down. He pulled a small whiskey bottle from the pocket of his jacket and took a slug.

'Almost time for the news, Lenny,' he said to shaven head, as if he owned the place. Shaven head was standing right beside me, his mouth clenched in an ugly smirk, his two hands rubbing restlessly against the shiny lapels of his jacket.

'We have nothing like that,' I tried again, my voice firm, my body in control. 'We're poor folks, with only our little house, perhaps a few pounds in my pocket, that's all. You can have that. But please go and leave us in peace. We have eggs . . .'

Shaven head moved. His left hand caught me by the front of my shirt, pushed hard against my chest, almost lifted me off my feet and I'm not a small man, pushed me back against the dresser near the back door. I felt the strength in his hard, big body. I knew the awful stench of his breath as his dark face came close to mine. His right hand was moving through my pockets, searching. He found a few notes in my inside jacket pocket. He held them up.

'Cash, Jimmy,' he announced. 'A few measly quid. 'Snot enough. Not enough by a long chalk.'

Woollen cap had sat back in my chair, the whiskey bottle in his hands. He lifted his legs and landed them both violently on the mantelpiece, shattering one of the china dogs, knocking off the candlestick and sending the statue of the Child Jesus clattering onto the small rug before the fire. It landed with a dull clunk and did not break. Woollen cap crossed his legs, keeping both feet on the mantelpiece.

'Sorry, missus,' he said, waving the bottle at Flo. 'Would you like a sup?' She stared at him. I noticed the boots he was wearing, how rough they were, unlaced, I noticed how a few drops of the whiskey spluttered into the air as he waved the bottle about.

'You can take the money,' I said again. 'Take it, but please leave us alone.'

'We can take the money, Jimmy,' shaven head said. Mocking me. 'Isn't he the kind oul' bastard. He's lettin' us take the few quid. The cunt!'

He pushed against me again, hard, back against the dresser so that it rocked and some of our old china plates fell off and smashed against the floor.

'We want more than a few measly quid, you oul' bollocks!' he shouted at me, his face right against mine, and I could see the red waters of anger in his eyes.

Woollen cap chuckled. 'Where's the savin's, missus?' he said. 'All the savin's. Just that, an' we're off. I promise. Just the savin's.'

Flo looked at him still with those dead eyes. I knew she

could not speak, nor stir an inch, her body stiff with fear and useless as a plank.

'Look,' I said. 'You can believe me. We have no savings. All our money goes into the hens and the eggs. This is all we have. Nothing more, I promise you.'

Ah but the shaven-headed man who held me began to shout into my face, to shake me hard against the dresser, back, forth, back, forth, plates fell and shattered, cups, saucers, and he shouted at me, the words so loud I could not make them out. Suddenly his right fist, clutching the banknotes, came hard against my face and I was pitched sideways and fell, my whole head an inferno of pain and noise, my hands grasping at the dresser to hold me, but I fell, lost, and breaking. The strangest thing of all was, as I lay against the back door between the old dresser and the wall, while the whole world was a thunder-storm about me, the Angelus bell rang out from the television set and automatically I began, somewhere down in my soul, the old and lovely words, *the angel of the Lord declared unto Mary* . . .

My head cleared quickly. I remember shaking myself, blinking my eyes, and then, from where I lay I saw woollen cap lift down his great boots from our mantelpiece and drive them both violently against the TV set. It smashed with a ter-rible clashing of glass and the set flew backwards against the wall. At the same time I saw poor Flo, incensed by the violence against me, loose herself suddenly from her terror. She rose from the table, I could see she was saying something, and then she was striding – yes, that's the word, even though she was an old woman – striding across the room towards shaven head where he stood in the centre of the kitchen. It was what I dreaded, this sudden anger she was capable of, that quick yield-ing to the chaos that is in us all.

She came up to shaven head and she pounded on his big

chest and I saw that right hand of his raised again. I screamed from where I lay, I heard the awful slap of his palm against her face and she was spinning away from him, and falling, falling, falling. I heard the dreadful thud of her brow against the raised stone of the fireplace, a woeful sound, dull and somehow definitive. She lay still, utterly, utterly still.

We began our hen run with some exotic hens, White Leghorn, Sussex White . . . but the poor things were quite unsuited to our rains, our chills, our backwardness. You cannot manipulate nature, you know; you cannot divert the river without consequence. So, eventually, we settled down with the usual Rhode Island Reds, and were rewarded, quickly and unstintingly, for our care. What is beautiful is the simple acquiescence to the divine order.

We were rewarded over and over again. So that we came to love our hens as if they were more than insensible creatures of flesh and bone, of feather and mucous-brain. At least I came to love them, even to name and know them individually, hen by hen, cockerel by cockerel. The day I realised that the onward-rolling world required we kill our first hen was a hard day for me. Flo laughed, mocking my theories and my grand words.

'Let them be pensioners, then,' she said. 'Let them multiply and lay, then let them grow old to eat the food and take the good from the young and laying, let the fox come and be a fox, let's wait for him to do the job for us, oh yes, but do not think a hen of ours can be killed and dressed for our own table!'

Flo was serious. I could see that look in her eye, that flinty anger, heating up. I went off at once and bought an axe. A good one. Strong and heavy and sharp. Flo and I together set up a little killing place around the side of the house, away from the coop, where we had a stone and could do the deed, for truly I had to agree, death is the necessary consequence of living and a well-cared-for hen is destined for the kitchen table!

Flo was good at catching the poor creatures, no-nonsense-Flo; she was good at holding them under one arm, at laying the neck out on our stone. I grew expert at the swinging of the axe, stepping in so fast that the open eye of the hen would not notice even the sheen on the edge of the axe before head and body were separated and another hen-soul, the body jerking and shivering, had entered her nirvana.

That axe, honed to perfection, I kept at the back door, just at the side of the dresser. Yes, you're right! oh yes, I'm afraid you're right. In the deep silence that followed Flo's fall it seemed that the silver edge of the axe, the smooth, light-wood handle, spoke to me more loudly than God himself would ever speak. I was wholly calm again, perfectly at peace.

Woollen cap had leapt from his chair and was standing, bent over Flo's poor spent body. I saw a pool of black-red blood beginning to spread out slowly where her thin hair lay on the ground.

'Fuck!' woollen cap said. 'Now we're in the shits for sure.'

Shaven head had moved away from me. He was watching down at Flo.

'Fuckin' not my fault, she came at me . . .' he was saying, but I was on my feet, I could see the small valley of the neck just above the top of his spine. I'm tall, you see, I was able to bury the axe so deeply into the back of his neck that his great, ugly eyes mustn't even have had time to blink, the axe came back out of his flesh and a sound like the gurgle of greasy water choking down a sink came from him. He fell, his hands like claws scrabbling the air and he lay, his body jerking and shivering on the flags.

Woollen cap and I stared for a moment into each other's eyes. Then he came towards me over the sprawled body of his companion. I backed away from him, towards the kitchen door. He came at me, yelling, determined. Just at that moment

I glimpsed my poor Flo again, the stockings tight under her knees, the flesh of her thighs, lumpy, exposed, holding her in an awful indignity. Woollen cap seemed to leap at me. I swung the axe again. I scarcely felt the impact but suddenly there was only a stump where his arm had been and he was screaming, he was on his knees before me, his body bent forward and I saw, between the dirty grey of his jacket collar and the dark wool of his cap, a small area of flesh at the back of his neck . . .

I love order, I have already said that. You will understand me now. It's after midnight. I'll phone, soon. A doctor would be of no use here. No. It's the police I'll call. Order has been rifled, the flow of the river outrageously dammed, there is nothing left me but affliction, and after the affliction – silence. I plead, therefore. I plead because I have done wrong, here in my kitchen. Let the foxes have the hens. But above all let the judges punish me for the few short days still left to me, let them have no mercy upon me for only out of such redemption can the beauty of the world and the perfect purity of my God penetrate once more into my soul.

A MIGRANT BIRD

The door opened and a draft of sour air hit Fonsie on the chest. He coughed his sandpaper cough and looked up from his low stool. A young man had come in, carrying what looked suspiciously like a guitar case. He wore a green baseball cap, turned peak to nape, a chunk of hair waving through the gap in front – like a crested grebe, Fonsie thought. A migrant bird, please God, for there was never a guitar stood up naked in Frankie's Hill-top Inn before. Cowshite! Fonsie said to himself, and bugger it!

The young man looked around the bar as if he had a mission. He wore a grey sweat shirt with *Up Yours* printed in purple lettering across his chest. A big brass ring was dangling from one ear. He had a small silver ring fixed in his nostril. Fonsie shuddered.

Someone had left another pint on the table in front of him, one of the Germans, probably, and he dived into its sweet black depths for consolation. He left the cream along his upper lip a while, then slowly drew his tongue through it, sighed deeply and left the glass down on the table. Fonsie, his face the grey brown of old harness leather, wore a black felt hat tilted at a challenging angle back over his head. He took a handkerchief from his breast pocket, folded it, tucked it and the tailpiece of the fiddle under his chin until everything was snug as a rabbit in its burrow. He lifted the bow and poured a long golden-liquid chord across the floor of the bar. The customers were bathed in honey.

Fonsie closed his eyes and took a deep breath. He began to play, slow-waltz time, two sharps, 'Rich and Rare Were the Gems She Wore'. He saw a large and generous bosom, rising and falling like a summer sea, he saw red and flowering lips, opening and closing on perfect teeth and a moist, welcoming tongue, he saw emeralds and diamonds and pearls and a tiara, rich as the lake of night that is alive with stars. He laid his head between those wondrous breasts and when he finished the tune he was resting by the hearth of a grand lord's manor.

The drinkers in the Hill-top Inn applauded noisily. Fonsie retuned his top string, twanging it close to his ear so he could savour it. The young intruder had drawn up a stool and positioned himself beside Fonsie. The old man sniffled loudly, took a long sweep from his pint, settled his fiddle again and leaped off the very edge of a high cliff into 'Bonnie Katie's Irish Reel'. He closed his eyes and giggled with delight. Didn't he know Katie well! Well? intimately! he would go so far as to say... well, didn't he chase her? round and round and round among the haycocks in Horan's lower meadows, over the bottoms, back across the lower stream, her laughter like the challenge of the skylark against a morning sky, her petticoats lifting about her till she fell, tittering and joysome, down among the shakings, and he fell beside her, his fingers skittering along the mearin's of her backbone.

When he paused he was startled by the wild clamour of applause that brought him back to the pub. He opened his eyes and there were people around him clapping their hands and smiling at him. He grinned, clumsily, and took the fiddle from under his chin. It was like taking a wedge of his jaw away, his empty mouth gaped after it, and he filled that gap with a long and cooling drag from his pint after his dry-throated chase around the meadows.

The baseball cap leaned in, suddenly: 'Old man, they kept talking while you played! How can you put up with that?'

Fonsie looked at him. He was very young, though big and handsome, in a sledgehammer sort of way. 'They do come here, sir, to have a pint an' a chat . . .'

'But how can they pick up the words if they keep chattering?'

'There's no words comin' from me fiddle, sir. I just plays.'

Fonsie dived for refuge into his pint. He finished it but kept the glass up against his mouth and glanced at the young man. He was reaching a big hand towards Fonsie; a large silver bangle clattered against a wooden one on his wrist. It was a strong wrist, covered with soft golden down, like a migrant bird's.

'Hi!' he said. 'My name is Brad Pinkleman. And yours?'

'Fonsie, Fonsie Conlon.'

'Can I get you a pint?'

Fonsie nodded. Anything to be agreeable, and he had journeys yet to make, across arid grounds. He closed his eyes again and set off, a fine ashplant in his right hand, a satchel filled with boxty bread in the other, and a paper-stoppered bottle loaded with Irish whiskey. He was on 'The Connaught Man's Rambles', out of Ballina and into Enniscrone, down to Sligo and beyond, to Carrick; a pause, in Dromod, for 'Peggie's Wedding', and then a dash to Castlebar where he dallied a while with his 'Fair Gentle Maid'. He leaned forward, his lips pouting, her lips pouting too, the space between him and her not that great, and closing by the second. He put his tongue out from between his teeth and as he did so he turned the corner into the last few bars of the tune, remembered he had no teeth, shut his mouth sharply and opened his eyes.

'I see you don't move up in the positions, Fonsie.'

It was Brad Pinkleman shouting into his ear, trying to be heard over the fine applause. Fonsie began his pint. The young man was drinking straight from a foreign-looking, long-necked bottle.

'No then, sir, I do shtop on this wan shtool th' whole time.'

'No, no, no! I mean you don't ever move your left hand up along the neck of your instrument, kind of limits your potentialities, if you know what I mean. Second and third positions. That sort of thing. See?'

'I do jusht play, like, you know. Sir.' Fonsie thought he'd lay it on a bit thick for this young genius. 'Sure you do only want to be in the wan position for "Fanny Power".' Fonsie chuckled and gave the migrant bird a playful dig with his knuckle-sharp elbow.

'I don't quite follow you' – and the young man lifted his bottle and took a long glug from the neck. Like a suckin' lamb, thought Fonsie. Brad began to unzip his bag and – to Fonsie's horror – a great yellow guitar was lying across his knees.

'Frankie told me I could try out a song or two, if you don't mind, of course. Might help to bring some of the younger generation into the inn, if you know what I mean?'

Fonsie was dismayed. He had played on Thursday nights, in this corner, on this stool, for over twenty years and had hardly ever missed a night. Holy Thursdays maybe, or when Christmas Day fell on a Thursday. But what could he say?

'Let Erin Remember...' he muttered, through his pint, a sound like stones stuttering in a mountain stream.

There was a big man standing over Fonsie, another pint extended out of the battlefield of the bar. 'For you,' the man shouted down at Fonsie. 'Ein pound of Guinness. Und can man hear *Die Koolin?* if I please? I come from Germany, no?

zis music pleases me very. *Danke. Danke schön. Und sláinte.*'

'As a Beam o'er the Face of the Waters,' Fonsie mumbled, grinning; Germans! they'd soon have every house in the townland bought up and converted; migrant birds, all of them, stretching the winter season into several years. However! and he stretched out his hand for the pint.

'How's the meadows, Fonsie?' someone called to him.

'They're lyin' down, Vinnie, lyin' down. Thank God for the man that invinted the silage!'

Brad drew a chord from his guitar and it fell onto the cement floor of the bar in a million pieces of shattered glass. Fonsie took a great swipe out of his pint and felt the cool hands within him massage his troubled soul.

'Fonsie' – the young man was leaning towards him again – 'what kind of an oddball name is that?'

The old man looked up at him. He was a looker, mind you, the young women would leap on him, surely. The way they never leaped on Fonsie. Except in his head, of course, when the music was flying. Brad had big candid eyes; the hands lying ready on the guitar were covered in fine, light brown hair and every second finger sported a ring.

'Alphonsus. It's short for Alphonsus. Fonsie. After the saint, you know. Saint Alphonsus.'

Brad, his brown hair down over one eye, knocked another row of bottles off a high shelf and began, in a strong bass voice, to sing. His eyes remained open, following the reactions of his audience.

'*Green,*' went the words, as Fonsie heard them, '*Green me a crew for the long voyage out, oh baby green me, green me a crew; yeah, yeah, oh baby yeah; flag me a wave for the long voyage out, oh baby lean on me.*' Then he knocked several rows of bottles off several rows of shelves, his head lowered and beating up and down to his rhythms, his lower lip clenched in his fine, calf's teeth.

'*Green me a crew for the long voyage home, oh baby green me, green me a crew; yeah, yeah, oh baby yeah; wave me a flag for the long voyage home, oh baby lean on me.*'

He has a good voice, Fonsie thought, if only he could find a song to fit into it.

When he finished, Brad seemed a little disappointed with the bemused applause that came from the crowd. But word would spread, his thews! his baby cheeks! It was between times, yet, between times in this backwash corner of the world.

'How's about you playin' "Danny Boy", Fonsie? and maybe I can strum along?'

Strum along! Cowshite! thought Fonsie, and bugger it! Yeah! But outside himself Fonsie smiled and tucked his fiddle back under his chin.

'What key's she in?' Brad asked.

Fonsie looked down at his bow as if the long curved timber held the answer. 'Two sharps,' he mumbled.

'Key of D. Right, old man, let's you and me strike up a storm for these innocents!'

Fonsie lowered his fiddle, reached for his pint and took a long, relieving scoop from it. Then he began to play, his eyes closed, his body moving proudly along from glen to glen and down the mountainside. He stepped out slowly onto a late summer meadow and Danny, young and eager and foolish, preening himself in his uniform of war, marched past him and away into the future. Don't be in such a hurry away from those who know and love you, Fonsie whispered to the brightly coloured back. But there was somebody at Fonsie's shoulder, moving with him as he flew into a valley all hushed and white with snow, there was a large presence, a bulked shadow keeping pace, offering to help him over stones, to open gates for him, to take his hand . . .

In sudden irritation Fonsie leaped away into the air like a

black cat pounced on by a dog and came back down running towards the 'Humours of Ballymanus'. This was better, he was free again, racing and cavorting round a noisy market square, in and out like a frisky pup between the legs of the cattle, nipping at them, teasing the big slow beasts while he whooped and skittered with laughter. He was joined by 'Paddy Haggarthy' and 'Nora Creina', and together they raced and frolicked, down side-alleyways, over gurgling waterways, tripping lightly along rough tractorways, back up the slopes and into Frankie's Hill-top Inn.

A great thirst had risen again within Fonsie's chest and he finished his pint with gusto.

'Well, old man' – it was Brad again – 'you could give Yehudi a master class any day!'

Fonsie presumed, because he was that kind of an old man, that this was intended as some sort of a compliment; he grinned his cave-mouth grin and licked the froth slowly from along his upper lip. He got up, stiffly, from his stool and made his way to the toilets, shouldering his way through the air thickened with gratulations.

Fonsie passed the new gents' toilet and went out into the yard where he had been going these past twenty years. He stood against the stable wall and sighed with satisfaction. The stars were beautiful overhead; there was scarcely a breath of wind. He felt a little dizzy and his chest was rough as a harrow. The world turns heavily, he thought, like an old, unoiled cartwheel. He thought he might give Frankie's a skip next Thursday night; the thought made him feel heavy as a haycock after rain.

'And if you come,' he sang it quietly, 'and all the flowers are dying, and I am dead...'

He turned back towards the door of the bar. As he crossed the familiar old rutted yard he heard the shrill high call of a curlew passing west over the mountain towards the sea. He knew it well, the curlew, he knew the lovely whirring sound its wings made through the night air, he knew the loneliness and the challenge both mixed into that local, endangered cry. He raised his head towards the darkness and smiled. He could hear the young man scattering his broken bottles about the floor inside. He giggled as another air came to his mind out of the darkness: 'Go Where Glory Waits Thee'. 'One sharp,' he said aloud, 'and up yours, too.'

He paused again, his hand on the latch of the back door of Frankie's Hill-top Inn. 'Brad!' he said to himself. 'Brad. What kind of an oddball name is that?'

FROM A WALLED GARDEN

I am going to write this down now for my own sake. For the sake of the self I will yet, one day, become. That I may read it again and remember. That once I touched on something, or that something touched me from beyond the ordinary gloom and boredom of the forenoons and the afternoons of my days. And changed me, utterly.

It was September the eighth. I stood at a gate in a high wall, up at the top of the town. There were wasps everywhere but I had no fear of them, nor of their purposes; they were obvious creatures, noisy and overt and deliberate. It was the harvesters I feared, blundering bodies like burnt-out matchsticks, those long, bent and wobbling legs that get caught in my hair, those shiftless wings that make a sickly whirring noise. And earwigs! earwigs I can never abide, their malevolent shape, their silent lurking, the bone-like texture of their malice! I shudder when they fill the early autumn days.

I stood a good while at the gate, savouring the moment. The gate was a thing of cabbage green painted iron, a blank eye in the high brick wall. Through the chinks at the sides I could glimpse only a sliver of garden, the edge of a footpath, nothing more.

'Pull once,' it was written. There was a short chain,

dangling. I pulled hard. I heard no answering tinkle from the other world. It was difficult not to pull again, difficult not to scream out for shelter and support. But I held myself stiffly. I was between worlds. I had already called out by tugging the chain on the bell. There would come an answer. I would wait.

At my feet I had all that remained to me of the world: a brown paper bag that Sweeney and Sons would use for filling up a stone of sugar. In it I had packed my things, underwear, twenty-four pounds in notes that I had saved from my years working in the stores, an old catechism from which I had learned to read, a brass crucifix that had been intended for the lid of a coffin, and a fine silver-inlaid dish that was a gift from the Sweeney sisters to the nuns.

Before the gate was opened I could smell the gatekeeper. There was an odour of sweat mingled with the must of advancing years, of earth and of the carelessness of dress. A male smell, disheartening and replete. I had expected the sweet arrival of a sister, whisperful, soap-and-dawn-scented, demure; but this was a clumping, muttering arrival, the gate's bolts being drawn back to the accompaniment of much eructation and some complaint.

There was a straining and grumbling of iron and then a grey, gaunt face peered at me from around the gate. I thought of the Great Famine, how the stress of starvation must have pressed the bones out through unresisting flesh, how the insupportable pain of watching others suffer must have turned the skin a hapless grey – and here he was, staring at me with rheumy eyes sunken in a cadaver face. I stood, my mouth open, and all words evaporated from me.

'Miss Sweeney, might you be?' he asked, and the voice was gentle, strong and strangely reassuring. I swallowed hard, and nodded, helplessly. The name would do for the moment; it had served, it would serve a short while still.

'Maybe you'd like to stay outside the gate for the rest of the week?' he mocked me, still softly, paternally. 'God can wait an eternity, young miss, but I've chores to do won't wait so long.'

He opened the gate widely and I got my first glimpse of St Agnes's, the high grey walls with their small windows, the tiny lawn starved for light between house and wall, the grey gravel pathway leading to the house.

'Please, miss,' he had to urge me again, 'pick up your trunk and come along.' He was already shuffling away along the gravel path. 'Shut the bolts behind ye, there's a lass,' he said, waving his arm vaguely at the gate.

I picked up my brown package and stepped inside. I closed the gate; it clicked softly but definitively. There were two bolts; I shoved them to. Then I turned and leaned back against the gate as if exhausted. He was moving away before me, his jacket grey and dirty, the sleeves too short, his trousers brown and hanging loose and low about him as if his legs were thin as posts and as if his buttocks did not exist. He seemed a ghost, a benevolent one, on whom the cloths of earth hung heavily.

I had not thought it would be like this, so empty, grey, silent, uneventful. And yet, what did I expect? the sisters lining the path? applauding me loudly as I strode in? an organ playing *The Arrival of the Queen of Sheba*? thuribles? incense? a bishop? God?

I laughed at myself and pushed myself from the gateway to follow the bodiless man along the gravel path.

I spent a morning in the washroom, out beyond the kitchens. There were two sisters, Raphael and Gabriel, gentle souls, elderly, slow-moving, sure. They did not speak to me. But all their gestures, their movements, their touches, were words more true than tongue could sound. I stripped myself naked before them. I stood on the cement floor in the middle of the washroom and Raphael, her habit brushing softly against my flesh, stood on a box and clipped my hair right down to the scalp. It fell about my feet, teasing my breasts, feathering its way down along my back, and I grew itchy and uneasy at its whispering reproach. When it was done the cold clean air touched my skull like a halo. Raphael got down off the box and her hands gently brushed the hair from my flesh, my breasts, my back, and once she lowered her head in humility and her hands swept softly down my thighs, behind my knees, and I could sense her gentle breathing on my skin.

I stepped at once into a great stone bath along the washroom wall. It was more like an old drinking trough for cattle than a bath. There were two taps opening from the wall and I turned them, cold water cascading down against the stone. I lowered my body into the chill water and felt my flesh thrill at the suddenness of it and my breath flew from me like a startled bird. Raphael approached and offered me a cloth of harsh design and with that I scrubbed my clean body cleaner still, working hard to make some suds from the bar of red soap she gave me, washing from my shaven skull to my heels while Gabriel looked on, and nodded, nodded, her eyes never meeting mine. I washed the world away from me in invisible particles of dirt and dust, cleaning the world's scents away, sluicing all of the past from my skin. Gabriel worked to sweep and gather up my hair. She took it all, and my clothes too, my skirt and blouse and cardigan, my shoes, and parcelled them in brown paper to give to the gardener for his fire, or to the almshouse for the poor.

I had a long, long journey to make. They sat me down in the postulancy room, all dark wood polished for so many years it had become darker still, a high window with a weak, angled light falling on Christ crucified. They sat me down in the centre of this little room, bare of all furnishings except for the low stool on which I sat; I was dressed in a coarse shift that pricked and scratched and chafed against my skin. They left me a while to pray.

But I could only sit, my hands folded between my knees, my bare feet cold on the polished floor. Outside, I knew, in the walled garden brown leaves were floating down like butterflies, pears were plumping to unnerving sweetness, the still-green leaves of the apple trees would be folding themselves up, like wings. There was a lovely silence in the room, the silence of peace and certainty, the silence of hope. I gazed at Christ the Crucified, the lover, his cross dominating the room; the alabaster body had gone grey with suffering, like the old gardener's skin, and the left side had turned the faintest madder-pink. He hung in silence and I longed for him, I longed to know such love as he had shown, I needed it, I was in thrall for it. His perfect face was turned away, turned towards the ceiling, the eyes were black and dulled, the countenance serene. To find such peace in the midst of all the grief that the human heart is capable of – there was a dream, an example, a call. I could not find my words. I knew I was a sinner. Unworthy.

The door opened at last. It was Mother Xavier herself, novice-mistress, inductress of postulants, exemplar. She was tall as a poplar tree, her body and face were lean and angular, that face all of a peep with the rigid sanctity of her habit. Raptor. I knew it at once, that sharp nose, that thin mouth, that intent gaze. Harrier. Eyes silver blue as a January sky. But there was a softness too in the eyes, a hint of sunshine, a knowledge I found restful and trustworthy and I laughed, a little nervously, when her talon-fingers began to wind around my head the long cloth that covered my scalp and fastened my mind to the

Lord. She wound it slowly, her long hands moving like a wizard's hands round and about my head, the coarse sleeve of her habit brushing against my cheeks.

'Stand, child,' she whispered, and when I stood she was neck and head above me, her chest flat as an ironing board and her smell as hot and cloyed, as reassuring. I lowered my head and she slipped over me for the first time the brown habit of her order. It was like diving in a dream into the dark and smothering embrace of the ocean, diving so slowly you feel the dream will never end. All was darkness, a rough brown darkness that brushed uglily against me, taking all my being as it enveloped me. I was clothed, my body hidden away, the weight of the cloth frightening me and the eyes of the raptor gleaming from her conquest. I laughed again, but I was hurting now, hurting in my whole self under that crude brown covering. Yet this was the moment I had longed for, dreamed about, imagined during all those years of fusty labouring in the world.

Mother Xavier showed me how to tie the wide black leather belt about my waist, how to gather the folds of the habit within it. There was a big and raw-wood rosary hanging from the belt. I could scoop it up in my left hand and kiss the frozen Christ on his crude wooden cross. I could shift the beads through my fingers with the greatest of ease. 'And Christ was on the rood.'

'Kneel, child,' she whispered, and when I knelt, the habit catching about my knees, and bowed my head, and when she leaned over me to drop about my neck the black and stiffened voile, my face brushed a moment against her cloth and felt the mothering caress of her body, like breast-feathers brooding over me, and the scent of her filled me with sadness for the entire world. As if it had to be this way, as if the world were no more than chimera and pain, as if abandonment and loneliness were all that we had to hope for.

'Your name, child,' she whispered.

'Angelica,' I said, and coughed, as the name seemed wrong; 'Sweeney,' I blurted out, loud and crude and filled with the things of the flesh and the world.

'Sister Angelica,' she answered at once. 'Sister Angelica. What a lovely name! Welcome, little sister of the angels.'

Then, quickly, as if she felt guilty for allowing herself even such a moment of simple pleasure, she turned and left me on my knees. I knelt awhile, upbraiding myself for not feeling that peace that I had longed for; the silence surged back about me, my breathing seemed loud and steady in that small space and my ears filled up suddenly with a harsh and ugly laughter that jeered and sputtered. But when I looked up and around for all those cruel mockers there was only the grey light from the window shivering high on the arms of the crucified Christ.

I walked often in the walled garden. For a time I found it strange to move, cumbered as I was by these new garments. It was solemn, and very safe. The walls rose high and the back of the convent, with its windows, its grey walls, its downpipes, its chutes, was intimate and reassuring. There were moss green spots of dampness on the wall, low down. There were gravel pathways among the flowers, rose beds, dahlias, flurries of late-summer plants.

Gus was the gatekeeper's name. He was everywhere about the grounds, coming and going between convent and town. He was everywhere, but you could scarcely ever see him, just a glimpse now and again. After his first scanted words with me there were no more. He was discretion itself. Gus, with his baggy trousers, and his corpse-like mien, his earthen aura, his somehow reassuring absence.

The novice-mistress had been reading to us from Thomas à

Kempis. Things like 'vanity of vanities, all, all is vanity', stayed in my mind. 'This is supreme wisdom – to despise the world so that you will draw ever nearer the kingdom of heaven.' I despised it all right. Hadn't I suffered, painfully but half-willingly, the attentions of the body of Big Bucko? That storm of sex and flesh and aggression. Walking on the garden path I knew I was in the right place. There were stone benches in the garden. Here and there. Well placed. I sat on one, close to an old plum tree. There were a lot of plums beautifully plumped and ripe, a soft flesh of readiness on them. I would have loved to gather a few and eat them. Because we did not eat so much in the convent, plain food plainly served, I felt a perpetual gnawing hunger in me that was to keep the mind from the things of the flesh. It would have been very wrong to pick and eat a plum. Around the base of the tree there was a great deal of fallen fruit, rotting now, blackening, earwigs crawling through and over them; wasps, too, a lot of wasps. I forced my head down to watch the earwigs, though I shuddered at their shape, at their colouring, at their gnawing.

There were butterflies. It was a while before I grew aware of the butterflies, dozens of them, resting on the plums, savouring the decay, the sweetness. The dark area under the tree seemed to be throbbing with them, with the trembling of their wings, leaving an impression of russet and gold with delicate patterning, like eyes. It was fascinating, beautiful. I knew how short their lives are, how they suck on such sweetness, shivering for a moment with life, and then they die. And we, drab human beings in our dull brown habits are born, too, to swell a moment with whatever sweetness we can find, and then die away into the air. Again I thought of Big Bucko and shuddered. We are born for annihilation and I had come to push that annihilation to the forefront of my being, and offer up all the sweetness in sacrifice. I turned from the butterflies and focused again on the terrifying bodies of the earwigs.

I trembled then in a sudden wind that had a premonitory chill of winter in it and it was then that I imagined I could see a shape shimmering under the tree, among the butterfly wings, the decaying plums, the few fallen leaves. There was a presence, not human, almost a light, a miasma, an angel; I believed it was a spirit of benevolence and promise, a whisper of love from God himself, a soft encouragement to me as I was setting out. The vision shivered a moment, hovering about the gorging butterflies and I felt myself falling sideways where I sat, falling with a pleasurable sense of weakness, the heavy brown habit softening my fall on the gravel of the pathway.

I remember seeing the grey-dusted boots, the grime-thickened trouser-ends, as Gus came scuttling along the pathway. I heard his muttering and complaining as he came towards me. I passed away into a warm dimness where soft lights moved. I was deeply, deeply happy.

'We are angels,' Mother Xavier said, her arms folded, her hands buried in her sleeves. 'We are angels. But we are fallen angels, graciously held by God from falling the whole way down to hell. We are caught in a middle kingdom, not all sorrow, nor all joy. We must fall back, labour after labour, into God's grace.'

She was beautiful then, there at the top of the room, dominating. I had missed some ten days, in the infirmary, oh nothing serious, a warning, merely; now I kept my eyes down but oh I was watching her, I was drinking her in, gathering her as a bee gathers pollen. She was rigid in her chastity. She was the blessed Virgin to me, intricate, and intriguing. She was my mother and I loved her. I kept my eyes down, but my soul shivered with delight.

How I envied her. She had achieved that late-winter bare-
ness that prepares a rowan tree for its fullest beauty. She seemed
to be gazing through and beyond us, her folded arms resting
on her pure, untroubled breasts. She stood, or sat, or knelt, but
all her movements seemed to leave her still as stone, as if only
her spirit stirred while the body was entirely an instrument.
Oh how I envied her, how I sat, fleshed, unstill, scared but
resolute.

I settled down into the gentle but exacting months of the
courtship of my Christ. We rose early, hefted out of sleep by
the clanging of the bell. We washed and prepared ourselves;
we gathered the darkness of our shadows off the back of the
cell doors where they hung and we tied them on. Swift as
mice, we hastened to the chapel, where, in the dim light of
candles, we sang our matins and prayed our prayers in the
sweet company of Jesus. It was hard, then, not to fall down
into sleep, for I was as yet too much subject to the demands of
my heaviness. But I was determined to succeed; I had not loved
my body, it had been abused, it deserved all the suffering I
could make it bear so that it could be cleansed and purified before my Christ.

My cell was home. It was small but it contained all I could
ever want. There was a window; if I stood on the wooden
chair and looked through the very top of the window I could
see over the wall out into the world; I could glimpse tree-tops,
fields far off on the side of a hill – and sky. After the first day,
when I did stand and look, I never looked again; why should I?
this was all my world now. There was a plain brown curtain
that pulled across the window. The walls were painted grey. I
had a bed, narrow and hard but adequate. There were three
hooks in the wall, one on the back of the door. There was an
electric light bulb with a grey shade. A low chest of drawers.
On top of that a delft hand-basin with a delft jug I kept filled

with fresh, cold water. A small radiator under the window that creaked and whined at odd moments. It yielded little heat, and that erratically. But it was ample. More than ample. For I had come to give up all comfort in this life.

We sang compline every evening and that was beautiful. The hours and minutes and seconds of our days were given to obedience and love but somehow the time of compline was given only to love. I was tired by then, it was a long day, loving was intense. I knew, with the incense fall of night, I would sleep blessedly. 'Now thou dost dismiss thy servant, Lord, according to thy word, in peace.' Oh it was lovely, like lying down into a dark wool cloud, music surrounding, the soul at ease.

When he created me he yielded up so much of himself until it became for him a crucifixion. So I prayed – let me, too, yield myself wholly to you, un-create myself again so I may give you back your entire freedom, your wholeness. And then we sang the 'Salve Regina . . .', oh the restful rise and fall of that chant, *'vita, dulcedo, et spes nostra, salve . . .'*

In the walled garden the world of nature had come to its necessary halt. Gus wandered about as if lost, appearing and disappearing from behind the gooseberry bushes, the blackcurrants, the roses. He was more obviously present than before, as if, with the fullness of growth, he had been obscured from our eyes. He fretted about the gutters and drainpipes, the gravel paths, the kitchen fittings, searching for labour.

I walked with joy in the coldness of the days. God, Mother Xavier told me, was extending to me the consolations of his love. Oh life was good, because life was being given back to the Lord. I would have sung my daily lauds in the garden, sung it out to the trees, the bulbs waiting in the soil, the grass stilled from its labour of growth. But I walked the garden, breathing out God's praises. There were rose bushes against the furthest wall of the garden. One bush was still in flower, though all the world else seemed dead and asleep. There were three perfect white roses praising the Lord from the depths of winter. I stood in rapture before them; they were a gift to me from God, a gift to me from the life I had chosen. Without thinking, I bent forward and plucked one of the roses and put it inside my habit to bring to my cell so that I could keep God's glory visibly before me.

That, I believe now, is where everything began to change. It was a sin to pluck that rose; it was a selfish thing to do for one who had taken a vow of poverty, promising that never would she hold in her possession anything she regarded as her own. Yet there I had the white rose, wrapped in moistened paper, lying on the windowsill of my room. A grave sin. A denial of the perfect love that ought to have been between my God and me.

I bent forward to inhale once again the delicious perfume of the rose when an earwig came scurrying out from between its petals. Oh that devil's shape, those awful curving horns like hooks, that desperate tail that twitched and attacked like a scorpion's. It hesitated on the sill a moment and I swept it down onto the floor at my feet. I stomped on it; I heard its carapace shatter beneath my sole; I heard its life squeezed out with unutterable violence and my whole being shuddered in horror.

Quickly I gathered away what I could of the tiny mess, rubbing with tissue paper against the stain, washing it out, cleansing it. But something remained, something of my sin, some stain that made a tiny part of the floor more bright than any other. I swept tissue and shattered creature together down the toilet. When I came back to the cell I could no longer see the rose in its innocence and beauty; rather now it seemed malevolent to me, reproaching me with my selfishness and my heartlessness towards one of God's own creatures. I gathered up the rose and brought it, useless, back to its flowerbed and laid it on the earth.

Compline that night was not easeful to me. There lingered some guilt in my soul that kept my eyes wandering about the chapel, that kept my thoughts butting against walls and pews and windows. I slept fitfully that night and somewhere in the deep blackness and silence I heard a faint scratching noise outside my window. I was high up, on the third floor of the convent, so the noise startled and puzzled me. I got out of bed, tiptoed to the window. The cell was desperately cold, the floorboards unable to retain whatever warmth the radiator had imparted to them during the day. The sound was constant and irritating and seemed to come from just below my window. I could make out nothing in the darkness. But I was disturbed and did not sleep at all for the rest of that sorry night.

Now soul and body were disturbed and my days were fatiguing and my nights broken. Oh of course I am no fool, I had put away all thought of rose and earwig, I had vowed again to my God to be wholehearted, always, in his care. I knew it was no great thing, it was a nothing, but the careful anxieties of our days, the disturbed nights and the long, prayer-filled, study-heavy days, were taking their toll. I had dreams.

I dreamed that the window of my cell had been quietly raised, that some creature, large and slimy and cruel beyond belief, had made its way into my cell and was waiting. That's all. Waiting. When I woke, again sometime in the bleak blackness of the night, I had to put my cell light on, check the window – which was closed and bolted – and search the room. There was nothing. Nothing. I sank more deeply into weariness.

In the early days of the new year the garden was locked away from us because of the rains and winds that raged down from the bleakest of skies. There were wild rushes of hailstones and flurries of snow. Some days were bright and clear with frost and it was dangerous to set foot on the world outside. We were weighted more deeply than ever in our prayers. I fought hard to find the words and consolation I had known. My body, too, though I tried hard to subject it to my will, was aching for ease and comfort. I fasted more and more, eating only a portion of the small meals that were given to us. And I laid myself down on the hard floor of my cell and offered the pain of my life to God so that he would come back to me and extend once more the hand of his love.

And then came that awful night. That dreadful night. I was cold, although I lay in the bed and had stretched my habit out over the sheets and blankets. I was cold and slept fitfully. There came again that faint scratching sound I had heard before. I tried to ignore it. But my eyes came wide open in the darkness.

I was certain that the sound came from just outside, and below, my window. I could not move. I was chilled through, my body tensed with fright. I tried to pray. The ritual words would not come. 'Our Father... Our Father...' No more. The thought came to me, one of Mother Xavier's phrases, *God is being crucified for love of us every day.* Somehow the notion, at that moment, made me want to laugh. But that was nervousness. No more. The sound persisted, a scraping at the base of the window frame. My life, I remember thinking, must be one of abdication, renunciation, pain. There was a sudden silence. As if something had been achieved. Or something had been abandoned. I lay, without breathing. Listening. I could put no name to what I feared. I lay, my eyes wide on darkness, my body chilled and tense. When I heard a sound that seemed to come from within my cell I almost screamed aloud for the loving touch of a friendly hand.

'I must suffer this.' I was forcing my thoughts, the way a donkey is forced along a muddied track. 'This is necessary for me. God's love controls the universe. Only by purification can I be worthy of that love, only by suffering and self-denial can I achieve that purification. Only by suffering this wonderful gift of God's grace can I achieve that acceptance . . .' I waited. The sound, soft, close, yet distant, uncertain yet sure, continued a while. I could not move. But suddenly, as I forced my eyes shut to undergo whatever was being asked of me, I felt a strong and sweet sensation across my body. As if a warmth of affection had breathed, like a summer breeze, across me. My being slipped into a state of anticipatory pleasure, the sound growing . . . seductive.

I waited, shivering with anticipation. The sound seemed to have ceased. I could feel nothing further. I waited. Nothing happened. I opened my eyes again with extreme difficulty, as if my body were weighted down with stones. I switched on the light in my cell. It was not long after midnight. There was nothing there. Nothing. The window was fastened. The curtain drawn. The door closed. There was nothing. I shook my head from side to side, mocking myself for a childish fool. I knelt at the side of the bed and forced the ritual words out into the air, whispering them, 'O my God, I am heartily sorry for having offended thee . . .'

I switched out the light. I got back into bed. I felt wholly exhausted and slept a thick, black sleep. It was dark still when we were wakened for matins and meditation. I drew back the curtains. I was exhausted. There was a faint glow from the walled garden outside. I would find the world sleeping under snow. How I looked forward to moving out there again, to seeing our wonderful enclosure wrapped and held in the purest blanket. As I turned from the window I noticed a wet patch on the floor of my cell. The boards, under the electric bulb, were darker in a certain spot than elsewhere. I touched the patch with my finger. It was damp. I glanced up to see if the ceiling was damp, if by chance there was a leak. The ceiling was pure and unstained. Perhaps some radiator pipe was leaking, I thought. I ought to have Gus examine it. But I knew I wouldn't say anything about it. How could I? How could I?

Those were difficult days. The convent never seemed to be warm. The corridors, the high rooms, the refectory, the kitchen, all were cold and damp. I was weary, too grateful for the vow of silence so that I could hold myself within myself and gaze into the mirror of my own soul and know its impurities. I nodded asleep during prime that day and promised myself to eat nothing at all at dinner time to punish my body for its sin.

I walked the garden in the afternoon. There were no other sisters there. The sky was still heavy with clouds. The convent walls looked wet and bleak, but the garden was a world of purity. Here and there I could trace the tiny lightweight patterns of small birds' feet. The branches of the naked trees were beautiful with a patterning of snow. The silence was special too, as if the whole world were a creature, subject to the necessity of God's caring, breathing quietly as it rested from its labours.

I came to the end wall. There were no roses now on the rose bush, the two remaining flowers had fallen dead and rank and there was nothing left of all the year's growth. It was a moment of panic as if now at last I was completely alone, without companion or comfort. I turned away quickly from the foolishness of my own heart. I walked around the perimeter path of the garden. There was a flowerbed under where my window would be. There was nothing there but snow. I looked for traces of any creature but there was nothing. The snow was pure and untouched. There could be no harvesters, not now, not at this time of the year, their scraping, reaching, terrifying legs would long ago have disappeared into the death of the year. I mocked myself again for my foolishness.

There was a pain of hunger in my stomach as I lay in bed that night, a gnawing pain that made me glad to be suffering for my sins. Oh I was evil. I remembered the great heavy body of Big Bucko, how he climbed on me when I was vulnerable, how he forced me to know his awful body. I shuddered at the memory of it. When I closed my eyes that night I could see him, swarthy, heavy, the dark and dangerous hairs at the base of his stomach, oh all of that came so vividly again before my memory that I knew once more that not only he, but I, too, had been guilty and unclean. And that was still a wall between God and me. And only the destruction of evil can leave the world clear between us, clear and beautiful in God's eyes.

I slept. Unhappily. In some pain. And in the very deep darkness of the night it began again.

I woke, sweating, in spite of the coldness of my cell. At once I knew it was that same soft, slooshing sound from somewhere inside my cell that had wakened me. This time I had no sense of fear, only a strange sensation of pleasure. I realised I had my fingers very close to my own body, that my rough nightdress was raised up, under the sheets and blankets, above my waist, that my hands were far too close... But I could not move, somehow, I could not move. I felt a strange peace about me, as if none of this were really my fault, as if it were wholly part of God's plan for me. And once again the image of the great naked and demanding body of Big Bucko came before my mind and my whole being trembled with anticipation, revulsion, longing. I breathed out heavily into the darkness of my room.

Still that sound persisted. I waited without terror. Once, I thought I felt the clothes at the base of the bed were being dragged down a little, but I could not be sure it was not my miserable imagination. Nothing more. Nothing but that sound as of something wet moving on the floor of my cell. I

jumped from the bed and flung the light on. There was nothing there, nothing, nothing. But that spot on the floor was just
a little larger, and when I bent to touch it it was wet, wet as if
newly dampened. I listened. But there was no sound at all
now, only the great silence of a dark disturbing night. I crept
back to bed; I left the light on; I heard nothing more. I slept.

During the restless days and broken nights of the dead part of
the year I suffered my darkest night. I spoke to no one of what I
endured. Sometimes the patch on the floor disappeared completely, sometimes it was larger and damper than before. The
sounds recurred, not every night, but often. Even the garden
offered no comfort; it too was dead, dreary and hopeless.

I knew that I was still old Angelica who had entered
through the iron door laden with the weight of living; I was
still that girl who had been abused by Big Bucko and who had,
at times, enjoyed the abuse and yielded secretly to it. I punished
my body the more; even on the coldest of nights I threw down
my coverings and allowed myself to shiver; I ate as little as I
could to sustain my strength; I walked still with my ego as
the great shadow that dimmed God's presence from my life.

And then it happened. Finally. I was exhausted. I felt I could
barely drag myself up the stairs after compline. I said my
prayers hurriedly, I fell onto the bed, worked my way in under
the covers and I slept. I fell into a darkness so black and deep
that it was comforting. And when I woke, somewhere in the
shallows of the morning, there was a pleasant soft light in the
room; there was a moon and the light through the curtains was
clean and vulnerable. I lay awake, not unhappy, just conscious
of myself, of my body, of the relief of even such a short period
of release. The sounds began again. I had learned to ignore
them, but this time there was also a scent wafting through the

cell. At first there was the dank smell of freshly turned earth, a slightly taxing smell, but pleasant. And then came the scent of roses, strong and firm and welcome. I closed my eyes and inhaled deeply and contentedly. At once I could feel that tugging at the end of my bed that had occurred once before. I opened my eyes. Something had come before the moon and the room was again in darkness. I heard a soft breathing in my cell. I knew there was someone, some thing, with me. But I had no fear. I offered myself to whatever God still took any concern over me.

For a fleeting moment the moon must have come out again and I saw, scattered over the walls of my cell, shapes that were lizard shapes, scorpions, harvesters, small, elongated, foreign, menacing. I was startled but the moon was quickly covered again and I was not sure if what I had seen was really there or not. I tried to cover myself in the bed. I noticed, vaguely, that my nightdress was drawn up even over my stomach and inadvertently my hand wandered down to touch the soft secret part of my body. I felt something fall softly on the bed, so gentle it was almost imperceptible. I pushed down the covers and there, in the faint moonlight, I saw a shower of white rose petals seeming to come from the ceiling down onto my bed. I shoved down the covers with a little cry of delight and let the petals cover my body. The scent was lovely, the room was filled with a delightful warmth and fragrance. I closed my eyes and inhaled deeply. It was then I felt the presence clambering over me on the bed and at once I remembered the great body of Big Bucko and how he had climbed onto me, taking his pleasure with me, causing me pain, causing me guilty moments of ecstasy. I kept my eyes closed for I knew that this was evil, this was something from beyond goodness or even human wickedness but I was too weak, I was helpless, I could not call out, I could not move. There was a body, naked and fragrant and heavy, moving with absolute determination over me, pressing me exquisitely down onto the bed, the roses and the thorns and the petals at once pricking me and softening his form. I knew, I admit it at once, I admitted it to myself right then, that I had greatly missed this nearness of a naked body, I had greatly missed the force and strength and presence, the complete abandonment I knew under the weight of Big Bucko's body. I yielded to the moment and I felt him enter me, there was a hot breathing over my face, great hands clasped me, between my sweating body and his there was a blanket of roses, rose petals, rose stems, and the pain was glorious and demanding. He entered me and I moved with him, I moved with joy and expertise and I held myself back for him as long as I could, I held myself back for my own pleasure and when I came I did so with a fine sigh of satisfaction and peace that left me exhausted, weary, spent, and immeasurably happy. I must have fainted away with the ease and release of it.

I slept. Richly, deeply, peacefully. I slept so well and so long that I missed the early morning bells in the convent and woke to an insistent knocking on my cell door.

'Are you all right, Sister Angelica?'

It was Mother Xavier's voice, concerned, cautious. I called out that I was all right, that I had a headache, that I would get up at once and go to see the infirmarian. But I lay on in the bed and only slowly did the memory of the night come back to me. It was only then that a terrible fear took hold and I sat up in the light of morning and looked about my cell. There was nothing there, no trace of a presence, no roses, no petals, nothing; even the stain on the floor seemed to have dried up completely. I began to fancy it had been a dream. I got up quickly and began to dress. I was confused. I felt well, better than I had felt for a long time. Outside my window the morning light was clean and bright; there would be the first hint of spring in the garden. I dressed carefully. I knelt by the bed and prayed to my God. But I knew the words were only words; behind them was confusion, fear, suspicion and for the first time a terrible sense of loneliness, as if there were in this world nowhere and nobody to whom I could turn.

The sisters had already finished lauds when I was able to join them. I prayed for a moment in the chapel and then went out quickly into the garden to breathe in the lovely air. Along the border near the roses, I could see the first slender shoots of the iris beginning to reach into the air. It gave me joy. Nearby there were the first tiny fingers of snowdrops and the thinnest suggestion of the arrival of crocuses. For the first time in months, I realised, there was a lift to my heart and I devoted myself wholly to the joy of the rebirth of the world.

I sat down on the garden seat I had sat on many months before and I eased my back against it. A sudden sharp sting caught me in the back of my neck and I reached my hand back as if there were a fly or wasp. With a chill again catching me, I picked a thorn out of the flesh at the back of my neck, a small sharp thorn, a rose thorn. I looked at it with incomprehension for some time. There was a hint of blood at the very tip. My body had gone cold and fearful again as if a severe north wind had passed across it.

For days then I lived as if only half-awake. I performed all my duties, singing in choir, chanting the hours, performing my manual chores, praying my prayers, with calmness and precision. But my heart was cowed, my spirit numbed. Tiny spots of eczema had appeared on my skin, on my hands, on my stomach and on my face. I withdrew even more into my own life, my prayers coming automatically and without force. I gathered up the words of our novice-mistress but they meant little to me. Until the morning when, shortly after my poor breakfast, I became violently ill in the small dairy where I was working. I had to fall on my hands and knees on the damp stone floor and I retched repeatedly and painfully. Afterwards, when my body calmed again, I lay prone on the floor for some time, exhausted, and I cried tears of loss and distress.

I must have been there for about an hour. I heard, noting them vaguely, the chapel bells call for the hours of prime, and terce, and sext. I let them pass. I was convinced that I was wicked beyond all, that I was doomed beyond what any human being had suffered before. That my unworthiness had been noted by my God who had abandoned me to the power of the devil, the devil who had wooed and tricked me. And I knew at once what I had to do.

Mother Xavier had said that the further we undo ourselves in the service of God, the closer to God we will become. We must *un*-create ourselves, we must suffer, we must not allow to the body any of its longings, we must even make it suffer for its needs. Now I knew that the only way I could hope to undo what I had allowed to happen to me was to un-create myself completely. To give myself utterly and without the possibility of reservation to my God in atonement.

I got up slowly from the floor. My body felt stiff and very sore. My habit was smeared with dust. I walked with determination back into the convent building. I climbed the polished wooden stairs. I climbed up, past my own third floor, up the narrow stairs that led to the storerooms at the very top of the convent. I knew that at the end of the room was a door, that that door led out onto the top of the old iron fire-escape; that there was an iron landing up there scarcely protected by any barrier; that there was a fine drop out onto the gravel pathway of the walled garden.

The door was locked. But I knew the key was kept, for

safety, hanging on a nail to the right of the door. I found it. I noticed that my hands were not trembling. That I was very calm and my body still. I opened the door. A sigh of very cold air touched me. I closed my eyes and accepted it. I stepped out onto the little balcony. There was a thin iron railing about waist high. I held onto that and looked over and down. One strong push and the iron rail would give and I'd be falling. I would become, for a second or two, just another particle of creation, like a stone, fully obedient to God's laws. I would fall, and break, and die. There would be nothing left between my God and me. I would be made perfect.

I breathed in deeply. I closed my eyes. I raised my head. When I opened my eyes again, prepared, I found I could see well out over the high perimeter wall of the convent. The day was a bright one. There were sounds of life coming from beyond our walls. I could see more of the trees that lined the avenue leading from the town to the convent. And away beyond, in a fair-green, I could see a market in progress, stalls, cloths of many colours, animals, the world animate and busy. Somewhere there was a bird calling out that it was spring. And on the horizon I could see white puffs of smoke from the engine of a train, smoke rising with an extraordinary calmness into the pure sky. It was as if I woke up suddenly. As if I had shaken some mist that had held me from my mind and heart and soul.

I stepped back, scared, from the edge of the landing. I peered down again and shuddered. Then I turned quickly, my habit swishing angrily against the jamb of the door, and went inside. I closed the door, locked it, hung the key back on its nail. Then I had to lean back against the door, and gather myself once more into calmness. I stood a long while, terror rising in me as I thought of what I had been about to do. I breathed deeply, deeply, deeply. Gradually a certainty struck me. I even laughed aloud.

I went downstairs slowly to my cell. I knew there was no mirror, not in any of our cells, not on the corridors, only out in the parlour where we were not permitted to go. I took off my heavy, clogging headgear. I shook out my hair which was beginning to grow back to its original innocence. I bathed my face in the cold water of the jug. Then I headed down past Mother Xavier's office. I couldn't resist opening the parlour door. The room was high and clean, bright with light streaming in from high windows. There were heavy, leather-backed chairs fixed precisely around a gleaming mahogany table. And there, at the top end of the room, was the mirror, oval-shaped, the edges bevelled and gleaming with silver. I watched myself a while in the mirror, knowing that all these months I had been gazing deeply into my own being with complete self-absorption, more than any woman could do who came to admire herself in the mirror of simple vanity. My face was pale, my hair, though growing, rough and unkempt. I bowed to the mirror, smiled and turned away to face Mother Xavier.

The next day, dressed once more in clothes like those with which I had entered the convent, I strolled slowly one last time around the walled garden. Everywhere there were signs of growth to lift the heart and make the body exult. Even the white rose bushes, though severely pruned, had long red and green shoots reaching into the air. I stood a long time, watching the dark walls of the convent, gazing up at the high landing from which I had almost spun my soul. Then, at last, I turned and went down to the old iron gate. I pulled the wire of the bell. Soon Gus came shuffling along the garden path towards me. He had not changed, Gus, still moving with a smell of sweat and age hanging about him, the smell of earth and of the dankness of unsunned places. He grinned at me. 'Miss Sweeney. Amn't I right?'

I only smiled at him, delighted as the name sounded once more in the living air of the world. He turned to the gate; there was a complaining of bolts, a straining and grumbling as he opened it. He held it and turned to watch me as I gazed one last time at the grim convent walls.

'God be with you, then,' he muttered, and there was a strained, knowing smile on that grey, gaunt face.

'God?' I said. 'No, sir, no clacketing, demanding, wizened old God, there will be no God, malevolent and self-absorbed and filled with bitterness, there will be no God at all with me from now on.' I smiled sweetly at him and turned, light and carefree, back into the world.

NIGHTHAWK

Reynolds walked home slowly from the supermarket. He had searched the shelves for parsnips and had lost his mind amongst kiwis and lychees, mange-tout and oak-leaf lettuce, mangoes, yellow peppers and out-of-season strawberries. The parsnips, too, when he did find them, were foreigners. They were forced, overfed, arrogant bastards. Too smooth, none of the clump of muscle, the crudity of limb, a lively parsnip ought to have. But he selected one. He laid it on the automatic machine and grew dizzy in his attempt to find *parsnip* among all the items pictured on the screen. A big woman, rushed and determined, her basket shoved into Reynolds's ribs, hustled him into action. He pressed the button for papayas and the sticky piece of paper emerged with a low whine. Two pounds and forty-four pence! He turned to the woman to offer an incredulous comment.

'God be with the good old –'

'Stand out, please, can't hang around all day, you know!' she barged at him before he could finish.

He left his parsnip back on its shelf.

As he walked home through the new estate Reynolds longed for wilderness. Each house along Heatherfield Heights jostled shoulder to shoulder with another. Each front garden was manicured and free of daisy, buttercup or thistle. The ground he walked on was concrete, without nettle or water-pool. Here and there was a black puddle left from the over-night wet dreams of cars.

Reynolds walked unhappily. His big body, made for farm labouring, was redundant around these crowded acres. His clothes, made for farm labouring, hung flabbergasted about his limbs. Sometimes he shaved, sometimes he didn't. Some-times he washed. If he could see a purpose.

People stepped off the pavement when they saw him come; the suburbanites; the dwellers in the land of Nod; they crossed to the other side of the street and engaged themselves in scru-tiny of pocket or newspaper. Reynolds was a focus for the black heart of Heatherfield. Scapegoat. Underperson. Fool.

He turned off Heatherfield Avenue onto Heatherfield Walk. It was quieter here. A young woman in jeans and sweater was outside her front door, rubbing hard at the letter-box. She paused to watch Reynolds pass, her head slightly turned to take him in.

'Day, ma'am,' Reynolds called. He lifted his cap a fraction, the way they used to do in the days of wilderness.

The woman turned back to her letterbox without reply. Reynolds imagined he could see the hairs on her back bristle with indignation. For a moment, watching the sensuous shape of her body bent towards the door, he felt chagrined. Then he chuckled to himself. Just passing the time of day, my dear, that's all, passing the time of day. Polishing up your gleaming letterbox. For the words that come from your own world, the bills, the insurance, the mortgage, the . . . Never was it known before that a few kind words of greeting went astray. Well, her loss, poor creature, only her loss.

As he passed the garden of number nine Heatherfield Court the burglar alarm went off with such violence that Reynolds leapt sideways onto the road like a kicked dog. He paused, watching the house. He could see no movement. Must have been a sudden breeze, a dog brushing himself against the patio window . . . The bell clanged on and on until Reynolds felt it shaking him the way a dentist's drill working inside your head will shake you to the hardened toenails inside your boot. He hurried on.

As he turned into Heatherfield Park, Mrs Amanda Willington-Leach came out onto the pavement from Heatherfield Close, pushing her pram before her. Holding hard to one side of the pram was the Snot Steven, four years of age, whose unbridled passion for throwing stones at Reynolds when the latter was up in his tree left the old man exhausted and disarmed. Poor Amanda! he hadn't the heart to tell her that her darling was a bollix. Amanda seemed to be a dear, not one of the Heatherfield set, she was without that turned-up face, that cautious turning-away of the head, those suspicious eyes. In the pram was a one-year-old bollix, Abraham, Abrahamfor-God'ssake! destined to be another skulking scorpion that would litter the floor of his peace.

'Day, ma'am,' he greeted, as he stepped off the pavement. She was pregnant again, too, how many would that be? five? boys! and Damien, her husband, determined to continue down the rabbit road until they had a daughter! Amanda was heavy, puffing before she had taken ten steps along Heatherfield Walk. Attractive, too, Reynolds had always thought, in a mayflower sort of way, alert and white and breathtaking for a short period because as soon as you looked again the mayflowers had all gone, leaving a labouring stem heavy with summer.

'Mr Reynolds, lovely day, praise God!'

How on earth could she say such a thing! the sunlight thickened with suburban dust, the heat of the day weighed down under the smell of oil and petrol fumes, the leaves of every tree leaden with urban fever.

'Grand, missus, just grand, praise Jesus!' Reynolds responded. He eyed the Snot Steven who was carefully holding his mother's skirts. If he could get his hands on the child... Reynolds stepped back onto the pavement; he glanced around; the Snot Steven had his ugly little tongue out at him. Reynolds noticed only the full-fleshed swing of the round buttocks of Amanda Willington-Leach as they moved behind the pram, shifting and beckoning under the stuff of her rosebud-patterned dress. Reynolds shuddered. Days like this the women of Heatherfield would be undressing, laying themselves out on relaxers and sunbeds, grilling artificially tanned winter bodies under the desert mercies of the sun.

He turned in at his own hobbled gate, admired the dandelions and buttercups in his carefully untended front garden, saw the long, purple bramble suckers reaching towards the immaculate gardens on either side, and knew some ease. Here, at least, he was free to cultivate his wilderness.

He pushed open the door; on Reynolds's house there was no alarm, no lock, no bolt, there never had been. Across the street Jonathan Hayes, young, hurried, taciturn, perfect, was polishing the bodywork of his new Range Rover. Reynolds watched him for a while; he was a saint, Saint Jonathan, patron saint of suburban sobriety; every second day he scoured that car, hoovered it, sprayed it, kissed it; but never once did he lift his head to acknowledge his doddery old, kindly old neighbour.

On into the afternoon alarm bells rang about Heatherfield Heights. Now and then a car alarm exploded, or someone locked or unlocked their car from a distance, and the car squawked obediently. Reynolds paced restlessly about his walled-in back garden, reduced over the years from bright meadowlands that waltzed under the breeze – corncrake-land, cuckoo-haunted, skylark-rich – to a wizened suburban plot. Beyond the gardens, cars, lorries and buses rushed over the asphalt as if every moment lost must be a gold coin lost, the hot wheels insisting: *time is money is money is time, time is money is money is time*. At Reynolds's feet the hens still clucked contentedly, scratching about in blessed unawareness that the world was closing in, shadowing their desert, cluttering their wilderness. And wilderness, Reynolds knew, was the only ground on which the great cactus flower of a man's life could hope to bloom.

He clumped upstairs and fell onto his bed, dressed still as if for farm management. Sleep was the way, a heavy sleep that would blot out the fuss and fustiness of suburban day. He would become an owl, a werewolf, a nighthawk, and stalk the darkness for that ancient quiet man must once have known. Reynolds slept, snorting and grumbling through his nose and teeth, while all about him the traffic circled like larvae, alarms clanged, screeched up and down the minor and chromatic scales of steel cacophony, while he dreamed baby dreams, sucking on the soft teats of absence.

Very late that night Reynolds took to his tree, the old sycamore that had been the pride of Heather Hill in the years of innocence, the one tree left in Heatherfield, shadowing his hens, its branches reaching out over the back wall and offering a distant memory of paradise to any passers-by who had time to sense the memory, suggesting the spaces of wilderness to those who could bear the strains of silence, the urgencies of magnificence, the reaches of the universe and the reaches of the human soul.

He sat quietly in his tree, his dark-clothed form merging with the dark heart of the tree's life, his body folding itself into a forking of branches. He breathed more easily; he was refreshed; he could inhale the night, without fumes of commerce. Something close to silence settled over Heather-field. From his perch Reynolds watched the lights go on and off in the back bedrooms and bathrooms of the estate. For one heart-stopping moment, Amanda Willington-Leach, heavy with life, stood in the afterlight of her bedroom window, her naked body straining towards the wilderness without. The orange streetlights scattered all over the estate vitiated darkness so that, standing solitary under night, the soul bursting to lift towards splendour, not one star would be visible throughout the heavens. Reynolds stared at the beauty of her naked body; he knew she, too, must be longing for the peace and space of the universe so that she could commune with that life within her. His body and his soul strained towards hers, strained out towards the planetary music of the night. Together, he and Amanda and the wilderness! desert fathers and mothers! they could wash their souls in starlight.

Abruptly, Amanda turned from the window and flipped the curtains closed behind her. Reynolds coughed, and spat, and wished he was a bird.

Only an occasional car passed now along the road. Reynolds's meditations began to grow more deep. He was back among the molten gold of the gorse-wild hillside, reaching among sa-cramental rhododendron purples of Heather Hill when his father perched him on the great shire horse, and he knew be-tween his legs the strength of boulders, the power of contained world-energy. His father showed him, naming them, the pas-terns, the feathered legs, the fetlock, the rump (oh lovely, lovely Amanda!), shoulder, barrel, croup, reins and bit and girth, all that – put together – harnessed a power close to the pulsing power of the earth herself.

A police car passed beyond him, slowly, its engine purring. Reynolds hugged the bole of his tree; he was almost at peace.

Here in the wilderness of night he felt he could achieve immortality.

Reynolds breakfasted at midnight. At three thirty he dined, a plate of puddings, livers, kidneys, and healthy scents floated like owls across the gardens of the estate. A walk, then, between the hours of four and five; he hummed to himself, the night belonged to Reynolds, and Heather Hill was abloom with the flowers of darkness. Then he climbed back into his sycamore and sat in peace until the early buses and cars set out from Heatherfield into the markets of the world. So, for three nights, Reynolds, werewolf, nighthawk, moth.

Late on the fourth afternoon he was awakened by a repeated rapping at his front door. He shuddered himself out of sleep and threw a winter coat over his pyjamas. Two policemen stood outside. Reynolds noticed that the alarm was hammering away on a house just down the road. Jonathan Hayes was in his driveway, shining the bonnet of his wife's Citroën MXD 800. His head lowered, in prayer.

'Mister . . . em . . . Reynolds?'

'Yes?'

'We have received several complaints about a peeping Tom in the area, and specifically, in your back garden. Sir. I am to inform you these complaints are to be investigated.'

'A Tom?'

'Yes, sir, a peeping Tom. And further to these complaints, sir, a tree in the back garden of number twenty-four, Heatherfield Park' – and he craned his neck ostentatiously, looked at the number on Reynolds's door, said 'H'mmmm', profoundly – '*your* house, sir, constitutes a hazard to public safety and an order has been issued to lop it down. You are kindly requested to co-operate with the authorities in this regard, sir.'

Somewhere in the green outback of Reynolds's soul alarm bells began to klaxon.

Jonathan Hayes had drawn himself upright and was staring directly across at the policemen. There was a fine smirk on his handsome face. For a while Reynolds stared back at him but he was thinking of Amanda Willington-Leach, of her phone and its delicate purring sound, like the self-centred purring of an old cat. He looked at the clean-shaven faces of the young guards before him. Up from the country to find jobs? Their hands were small and manicured, their uniforms spotless, their buttons a-gleam with authority. Outside the tumble-down wooden gate of twenty-four Heatherfield Park their forget-me-not-blue car waited; they did not do their rounds, these men, on black High Nellies.

Reynolds plunged. 'Well. Do you know what, now, guard?'

'Sir?'

'I've got a sudden urge on me to buy myself a feed of man-goes and kiwis and quail birds. If you'll hold on there a minute, you might give me a lift as far as the supermarket?'

Across the road, Jonathan Hayes, seeing his own face re-flected in the bonnet of his car, smiled towards the world of reality. Heatherfield Park, he said to himself, is a watering-hole, a waiting-room, a foyer; soon he and his wife, the shining Sylvia, and their one child, Jon, would move into a five-bedroomed, detached dream-house over in The Orchards. Oh yes, he had a fine future ahead of him out beyond the perimeter of Heatherfield.

TWENTY-THREE

It was scarcely dawn. She got out of bed, quietly. She was frail, light as a bubble. Made no noise dressing, easy to dress without care or attention to details, to colour, to effect. Left the room, opening the door softly; then paused, glanced back at him, and for a moment remembered the lift of the heart towards joy that she had sometimes known with him. She wanted to go and kiss him, gently, but dreaded he might come awake and balk her of her purpose. She lingered, watching him; the stillness of complete sleep, how restorative it must be, how grateful she would have been for it. What her purpose was this morning she knew, and did not know. But at least she had a purpose.

She turned and closed the door, cautiously, behind her. Like the crossing of a border, a line passed over, and no return possible. She stood, leaning her back against the door, watching across the little hallway to the closed door of her daughter's room. The child would know nothing of all this, hardly a memory, except perhaps of a slender, blue-dressed woman who had held her so fiercely once that she had to cry out from the demanding excess of it. She would remember some moments of sunshine, speckled shadow on a small garden, her task of running between father and mother with little messages of love.

The day he had worked on those gorgeous, ridiculous sun-flowers, and she stood at the window, preparing something, a lunch, something . . . and watched him; the child played at the borders of a hedge, toys ranged about her, a goddess ordering her world, talking to herself, laughing. Had caught her mother's eye, had run with the message, tell him I love him, and she had laughed, tugging at his shirt and told him, and he had turned towards the window, the spade held high, the silly green wellingtons, and had laughed towards her, and then the child had come running in with the message, he loves you too.

Early sunshine was slanting in through the coloured glass of the front windows. The house looked east, towards the sea; the sun was weak, but promising; green and red light through the stained glass around the door lay across the wall. She was young yet, old as the sun. She opened the door into the kit-chen. Here it was still dark; she drew the curtains and looked out onto the meadows at the back of the house. There were two large hares sitting on a dirt track at the edge of the mea-dows. Once her heart would have leaped to the beauty of their fine, brown bodies, ears cocked, and she could become *voyeuse*, tender, longing to befriend them. But they too were on the alert, threatened, gentle souls.

She turned to the kitchen; the table was laid for breakfast; three places, prepared for another day. The small round plate belonging to her child, brightly coloured patterns of mouse and buttercup, hurt her. Delicate things, despised and threat-ened, the way the world falls heaviest on the frail, on the unresisting. On the mantelpiece stood a cheap, shifting calendar, the round face like a miniature clock, and when you turn it the day's date comes up. She turned it, knowing well, yet dreading . . .

Twenty-three. There it was, black on white, twenty-three. Two, three. Twenty-three. 23. She whispered the number several times in the small cell of her mind. Then she sighed deeply and turned away. She knew he would not have turned the date, not today, not to 23. As if, by not mentioning the date, it could be glossed over, ignored, avoided.

She cannot eat; she is too lethargic to boil the kettle for a cup of tea. Instead, standing at the sink beneath the window she pours herself a glass of water. Already the two hares have disappeared, the way happiness disappears, leaving nothing behind, no trace, no marks, only faint memories and the heaviness of its absence.

She sipped from the glass, poured the rest of the water down the sink. Carefully she replaced the glass on the draining board; she had been breaking so many things recently and today it was inevitable she would break something, break, destroy, defile. Above all she did not want to wake him, he would question, telephone and the whole terrible routine would start all over. Spare him, spare herself that. Today. The twenty-third.

Quickly she unbolted the back door and went out into the bracing air, the brash light of morning. They say that the berries of the yew tree will give release; she has never tried. Others, yes, others. Other ways out of this valley. Around the side of the house, a chill dawn wind taking her, gripping her flesh through the light cotton dress, a fawn field with a summer of tiny blue roses. Around the front of the house, down the path, out the old black gate, onto the road. Turn left, take the estuary path. And go.

I remember the first time. He was out. I was putting a face on things, a body on things. But I was already a ghost. It was the twenty-third. Of course. He was at work, elsewhere. I was alone. It all came upon me the way it has been lying for the last days, weeks, months perhaps. How hard it is to remember spans of suffering. They seem to merge into one restrained, long scream. I phoned him. Desperate.

'Can you come home? Please come.'

'I'll have to ask to get off. I'm on my way. Are you all right?'

'Yes, I'll be fine, soon; but I need you, now.'

He was on his way, that was something. I stood looking out at the street, then, in that old house, our first, filled with ghosts and agonies. I had to hold on to the jamb of the door. Ghosts. From where? who knows? But they're there; all the deaths, tears, heartbreaks, we breathe them in, they flood into my soul, weaken my body, grip my will and squeeze it dry as cardboard. He is on his way. Twenty-three. I may have caused him to lose his job because of my foolishness. I have to clear his life of me, cause him deep suffering for a while, but that will ease away and he will be left with happy memories, of love, of days running on the beach, of laughter, the comic relief offered us now and again in the ongoing tragedy. The mind sifts, for its own survival.

That day it was the gas oven. And of course it failed, because I did nothing to stop the gas from getting out, out the doors, out the windows. So that when he came back he found me laughing, the house reeking with the stench of sweet gas, laughter that was worse than tears, and we fell to the floor together, he in an ecstasy of distress, I pleading with him to grant me relief. The round began once more, hospital, tablets, lectures, restorative pointless work, the weaving of baskets, the colouring of cards, all over again. Twenty-three. 23.

★

To her left as she walked stood a few houses, blinds drawn, no smoke yet from the chimneys. Somewhere the sound of sea-birds, the long trilling of curlews, the bickering of gulls. Their life easy, a matter of moment to moment, grasp and eat, mate and die. There were boats drawn up along the grassy shore of the estuary, drawn up and overturned, weighed down by ropes and stones. Carapaces. Dead. At peace.

Further to her left the sprawling meadows, filled now with daisies, grass swelling and rising to the mower, buttercups, clover, early sun slanting over all, breezes moving it as a dress would move in a slow dance. She laughed. She would have been a dancer, swaying, rhythmic, the movements of arms and legs, of hips, shoulders, the moving of the whole body that merges with the great swing of the world, in the dance. And he, poor soul, he cannot dance for grass-seed; stands shame-faced, self-conscious, moving against the rhythm, stiff as a post. But, like the boats, like the gossamer soul balked by bone, she could not dance, not now, not ever again.

What her purpose was this morning she knew, and did not know. To her right stretched acre upon acre of mud and silt and bubbling ooze leading to a channel where the great river flowed; sometimes the tides overreached and swans came floating down the tarmacadam, she had seen buses come through with difficulty, leaving a wake behind them like a ferry makes over the sea. Then the world was beautiful, smooth as a desert, full-breasted down to the mouth of the river and the ocean. Now the tide was out, the mud shone silver in its wetness, there was even a green film of growth nearer the road. And out beyond the furthest wall of boulders runs the great channel, deep and fast, rushing out into the body of the universe.

She stopped. Three mallard came flying low over the estuary towards her, out of the sun. They moved faultlessly along the air then veered away. She heard the pounding of their wings as they rose together again, turning sharply seawards. Together. Sharing everything. Perhaps... perhaps he would wake, come after her, stop her...

She moved, resolutely forcing herself to carry on along the road. Around the turn, towards the little village church. If she could reach the church... It would be open, even at this hour. Out here, at the edge of the world, it waited for such as she to come in out of the anguish of the day, for such as she, poised on the end of the pier, ready to fall. Perhaps, if she called out again, deep within her soul, soundlessly, he might hear through his sleep, and come, the door at the back of the church would open, she would turn, he would be there...

That other time, when he came downstairs, he said something had moved him in his sleep, and he woke and I wasn't there beside him, it was not yet dawn, and he knew, with an instant and absolute certainty. He came downstairs and found me, at once, I was sitting on a chair in the kitchen, I had taken a full glass of weedkiller, the plastic bottle with the childproof cap, I had read the label, it had the skull and crossbones and the lovely word *Poison* on it, I had taken a full glass, it had tasted normal, like water, except perhaps a little salty, something like chlorine, and something else, remote and searing. Peace. That day was the twenty-third, too. He shook me, bodily, I think he was shaken by my quietness. I smiled gently at him, I was tranquil then, it was over. I said 'Good morning, love.' Because I was on my way then, on my way, as you would ease into a longed-for holiday... On my way.

He saw the bottle, he picked it up and he knew at once. Tears began to come pouring out of his eyes, immediately, so that he could hardly read the label. That was too much for me, for my peace. His tears. For me. I could not go with that. I could not. I had read the label, carefully. I ran to the tap, poured glass after glass of water, and drank it, drank it down, glass after glass, I had read the label, I retched and retched and I got rid of the stuff. And then, of course, the round began once more, the doctor, casualty, the hospital, the asylum, six weeks here, six weeks there, until I came back into the world again, reconstructed, held together by the wires and glue of tablets.

She reached the door of the church. Beside it an old cemetery, rickety, filled with nettles, high grass, montbretia, thorn bushes. The headstones lazed in the early sunshine; she watched for a while, then turned and pushed open the door of the church. The tide so far out. The walk so horrible, all that mud, that mess . . . But if she failed this time! no, not this time. She could not fail this time. It was the twenty-third. This was the final twenty-third, the one all the others had been pointing towards.

Even as a child she had hated the number twenty-three. There was a man, a stranger, called to the house once, and stayed up in the box-room at the angle of the stairs. He was big, that's all she could remember, dark-suited, and he patted her a few times on the head, but she hated him; he was more a shadow than a person, spent hours in the drawing-room, closeted with her father. And once, when the others were away, he took her and put her on his knee and his hands touched her and she felt ugly and ashamed. She was outside the door when they came out; he was loud, laughing, her father was quiet, restive; again he patted her and she could see her father frown. Then he was gone. For some reason, the way he bent down over her, like a huge shadow engulfing her, the number twenty-three, 23, always reminded her of him.

Ridiculous! Of course! But there doesn't have to be a reason for such obsessions; they are, and that's all. She sat at table twenty-three at her brother's wedding. That day she cried and cried, and had to reassure her brother that she was truly happy for him. And the day she fell under the bus! that was the twenty-third, too, when she ran out from behind a car, her own fault, and the front of the bus glanced against her, patted her, she fell, scars still on her lip, on her leg. Twenty-three, stalking her, waiting.

What was this he said? if you ask your father for bread do you think he will hand you a stone? Christ, too, I forgive; I forgive him for all the stones he handed me, for the love he offered us, forgive him that he made us kill him, for our safety, for our freedom.

She sat alone in the church for what seemed an endless time. Yet her watch still said only twenty minutes to seven. A low buzzing at a window distracted her; a bluebottle, wearied from its attempts to find a gap in the glass, to escape. She opened the lowest part of the old opaque window, and waited to see if the fly would discover its freedom. It stayed motionless on the sill. She whooshed it gently; wearily it rose and buzzed for a while against the rim of the glass, found the opening and was gone.

Very slowly, as if dream-walking, she left the church. She turned back, along the estuary road, towards home. She moved now without willing it; she moved as if entranced. The tide was rising, little rivulets moving in along the mud. She stepped over the low wall onto the grass verge beside the estuary; the grass was salted scrub, branches of dried-up weed littering everywhere. There was a low groin, a wall of boulders leading out from the road towards the channel; the boulders were covered in seaweed, dry in the early morning breeze. She began to make her way out along the groin, climbing carefully. Here and there the rocks were buried under mud and her feet sank in the nauseous stuff; the noises of gurgling and shifting muck reached her but her determination had grown and she ignored her distaste. Once her right foot sank in mud almost to her knee; she leaned against a rock and had to drag her foot out, leaving her shoe somewhere down in that black horror.

To her right the tide was moving in; behind her, already, a fast movement of salt water had covered part of the groin; dawn chill was leaving the air; out here the breeze seemed almost gentle, an easy warmth caressing her. Above her head somewhere in the silver sky a lark was trilling. She heard it and paused, listening. But quickly the sound of the rushing water in the channel took over. There was a sudden surge of panic in her soul; she quietened it; no more thought, now just a steady going with the will of the world.

She reached the great restraining wall. She stepped up onto it and saw the channel; below her, water of the incoming tide clashing with the downrush of the river, creating a maelstrom of seething, clutching power. The noise was almost deafening out here, the water deep enough to carry great cargo ships. All she had to do now was drop, allow her body to fall forward and it would be over at last. All over. Yield to the drag, the ever-present drag, of the darkness that had haunted her, had isolated her from living, had kept her body and soul from joy.

Once more she turned, to gaze back across the estuary to the road; she saw the tide already covering so much of the mud and boulders she had traversed; now the same rushing seething water had drowned the greater part of the groin; there was no way back. She gazed towards the clump of trees behind which was her house, where he still slept. She looked at her watch. Scarcely an hour had passed, an hour that felt like a lifetime. He slept, he would sleep more easily, she would sleep perfectly, at last.

As she turned back to the channel she saw the early morning bus from town turn the corner of the estuary road and approach the village. The sun gleamed off its red body; she could hear the ordinary sound of it, she could even make out figures sitting by the windows. The bus dipped with the road, disappeared into a hollow near the bridge, then reappeared, closer to the village. Soon it would pass their house. Later on, their child would be standing out on the road, waiting for the next bus that would take her to school. Alone. Lonesome perhaps. Hurting. She paused. Hurting? She found tears in her eyes; she was crying, a flood had been released. She called out with the relief of it, she had not been able to weep for months, her soul had been dried as a twig. She wept, for herself, for her daughter, for her husband; she wept for the beauty of the world.

One of the passengers on the bus stated that he had seen the figure of a woman out on the restraining wall of the channel. He was surprised to see anyone out there, especially at that hour of the morning. He had watched, filled with curiosity. She seemed to be struggling on the top of the wall, hands waving in the air; he thought first that she was waving to the bus, then he believed her to be in some sort of trouble; she seemed to try to climb down the wall but between her and the road there was only a heaving sea of water; she had appeared to slip, to fall against the stones of the wall; vanished out of his view into the river beyond. He had had the bus stopped, they radioed for assistance. But what could they do? She would have been swept at once into the maelstrom of that river.

BIG LIL

She got off the big green bus at our crossroads. I was sailing a ship down the drain outside our house and the whole day had gathered to a hush about me. By the time I noticed the CIE bus it was grinding down in gear, preparing to stop. The conductor got off, the envied ticket-machine fixed on its straps and belts around his fat belly, the brown, frayed satchel for the coins hopping off his hips.

'Hup, ya wain ya!' he threw towards me, winked and began to climb the ladder at the back of the bus. Then, suddenly, the whole day disappeared down the drain before the pressure of Aunt Lil's appearance. I forgot bus, sunshine, ship, conductor. Aunt Lil was big, dressed from toe to bun in daffodil yellow. She came upon me like a storm.

'Hey! you puke you! You must be Henry!' she thundered down at me. 'My my my oh me me my! how you have grown! You're a regular fairy now, a fairy, bless my soul!'

And she gathered me off the earth to the mountainous reaches of her chest, slobbered a wet kiss on my cheek and overwhelmed me with talcum powder. There were two large suitcases standing near our gate. She wasn't passing through.

For days then, she was loud about our house, her laughter echoing in every room, the woodbine scent of her presence lingering, astonished at itself, in every alcove, up and down the staircase. The house shrank before her and grew crowded. She would stay a month and we would have *oh such mighty fun!* and wait till you see what I've got for you, Henry! – it is Henry, isn't it? and what a funny name you've got, Hen-*ry!* (rising in pitch) and she laughed and would not listen when I told her my name was *not* Henry, it was Tim-short-for-Timothy! – what had I got? a pair of woollen gloves with no fingers in them! all the rage in Ballina, all the rage! Mittens, she called them, white, with little red flowers on them! For girls, I knew – and anyway wasn't it spring and nobody puts on gloves in spring, the cold, finger-nibbling days were over. I hid them away in a drawer upstairs.

Then one day I was reading a copy of the *Dandy* in my cave under the stairs when she poked in her head and scent and roared: 'Henry! you'll go blind in there in the darkness, boy!'

'My name's not Henry, and your name's not Lil!' I retorted. She laughed.

'I heard Mammy call you Lily, and once I heard her call you Lil-Lil!' I struck again.

'My name *is* Lily,' she answered me, quietly enough. 'I was born on Holy Saturday and they were gathering lilies for the chapel so they called me Lily. Lil is short for Lily and when I was small' (was it possible she was ever small?) 'they used to call me Little Lil because my mammy was also called Lily and so I became Li'l Lil. Now, Henry, does that satisfy you?' and she laughed and vanished, like the dinosaur in the tale of Mucker the Pig. I had learned something from her; she had learned nothing from me.

That night I couldn't get to sleep. There was a party on downstairs, an adult party. The adults often came to the house, to sit around the big table in the parlour, have drinks, play games of poker and chat about the world. I kept hearing the laughter, the murmuring of voices, the tinkling of glasses. I crept to the top of the stairs, saw the light under the door below, crept down further, and listened.

These were the lonely ones, even I knew that: Father Blackwell, the widow Claine, Helen Blair, the old spinster schoolteacher, Harry Weir, the retired doctor, widower. Good sports all, especially our Aunt Lil in her daffodil yellow suit. Our exotic bird.

I was sitting on the bottom step, my face against the banisters. I imagined I was an Indian, imprisoned by the cowboys of Tombstone City. I heard Aunt Lil's laugh rise like a sudden pheasant out of grass and I thought for a moment how wonderful it must be to be a grown up, to know the world, to hold it up to the light like a shining goblet filled with golden liquid, when suddenly Daddy gathered me up from there; you could have fallen down the stairs, he said, not scolding me, and I asked him how you could fall down the stairs from the bottom step but he only said not to be clever and I was asleep before I could answer him.

'What's whiskey like to drink?' I asked Aunt Lil.

'Well, well, well, the child's a regular fairy!' Aunt Lil said to my mother. 'You mustn't ask questions like that, Henry,' she said to me. 'It's like fire. It can burn you up inside and set flames going in your head.'

I found a pool further along the drain where the water came rushing through a pipe under the road. I ran between pipe and pool, watching my ship disappear and reappear and settle into a slow waltz in the pool. It was fun. Suddenly Father Blackwell was a dark cloud above me.

'Hello, Tim.' He smiled down at me out of the great height of his blackness.

'Hello, Father.'

'Is your Aunt Lil inside, Tim?'

I watched him stride through our gate, cross the yard and go in through the back door without knocking. Father Blackwell never knocked. He was too important. It was as if he was permanently expected in every house. I ran in to see what was going on. Aunt Lil was in the kitchen, sitting on the edge of the table, her legs crossed, swinging one leg. She hopped off when she saw Father Blackwell and wanted to make him a cup of tea.

'Give him a glass of whiskey, Lil-Lil,' I said, bold as buttons, in an attempt to put her in her place. But she only blushed and lowered her head.

Father Blackwell took me by one ear and pulled me out the door and into the yard. My ear hurt. My dignity was appalled. 'Out, Tim!' It was an order. 'Go and play in the forest with the big bad wolf! And keep your smart remarks to yourself or I'll put ten wasps buzzin' in your lugs!'

Oh I was sore! The indignity of it! marched out of my own house by foreigners!

Some days later I was again roused from my hiding place by Mother calling me indoors. I was to go on a message to Father Blackwell's house.

'It's Grandad's anniversary,' she said, 'and I want Father Blackwell to say a mass for him on Sunday.' She rustled in her purse, pulled out a ten shilling note.

'Ten shillings!' screeched Aunt Lil, who, of course, was about. 'That's a great heap of money...' and she followed me out the back door as far as the gate. I was tensing myself up to run when she called.

'Henry, like a good lad.' She was speaking quietly and I was stricken by the way she glanced about her. 'Give Father Blackwell a little message from me, will you? And I'll have a penny for you when you come back. Tell him... are you listening? Tell him *my resistance is low*. Do you have that? Tell

him Lil says *her resistance is low*. Off with you now.' And she
chuckled a big, daffodil-yellow, bosom-shaking chuckle as I
sped off, murmuring the phrase to myself.

I was scared of Mollie Quinn, the housekeeper. I knew she'd
be in the kitchen at the back of the presbytery so, against
unspoken rules, I knocked softly on the front door. Father
Blackwell himself opened the door and I blurted out the re-
quest for a mass for my great-grandfather's anniversary. I
thrust the yellow ten shilling note towards him.

'When did your great-grandad die, Tim, do you know?'

'It was in nineteen oh two, Father.'

'Nineteen oh two? Well now, take that money back to your
mother and tell her I'll say a prayer for him on Sunday during
mass and you can tell her, too, that your great-grandfather is
either above or below by now.'

'And Aunt Lil sends a message, too, she says to tell you her
resistance is low, Father.'

He seemed startled. Then he grinned. 'What was that again,
Tim?'

'Aunt Lil says to tell you her resistance is low, Father.'

He laughed. 'Right!' he said, 'for that you deserve a biscuit
from Mollie's special tin.'

That was the last thing I deserved, Mollie's biscuits always
being soft as damp paper because she never left the lid on the
tin properly. The oul' heap!

The poker games seemed to become more frequent in our
house. Sometimes there were only my parents, Aunt Lil and
Father Blackwell. Aunt Lil went around the kitchen a lot,
humming some song or mixture of songs but, whenever I appeared, she always brought around whatever melody she was
torturing to end up with, '*My resistance is low*.' Then she'd look
at me and laugh.

'Lil,' she used to say now and then, 'L – I – L. Lil. Large is luscious. What do you think of that, eh Henry?'

I had to fight. 'L – I – L. Lil. Large is lumpy,' I offered. But she only haw-hawed!

Time passed. Aunt Lil asked me if I'd go and live with her in Westport. Trying to be funny again. I agreed at once and she told me I was a fairy.

'Shall I go and pack, Aunt Lil?' I asked her innocently.

'Do, fairy, do!'

I went upstairs and got my toothbrush from the bathroom and my chamber pot, the chipped white one with large fuchsia flowers painted on it, from under the bed. When I came down Father Blackwell and Aunt Lil were chatting in the kitchen. I interrupted something.

'I'm ready, Aunt Lil,' I said, holding up my baggage.

'Well, well, well,' she tried, but her voice was forced. 'The child's a regular fairy, Father Blackwell, he's a fairy.'

'The child's a regular slug in the cabbage of bliss!' Father Blackwell hissed at me and once again I was taken by the ear and marched out of my own house into the yard! 'Out you go now and play with the bears in the woods where all little children should be or you'll have a swarm of bumble bees a-buzzin' in your lug!'

I put down my luggage outside the door. Then I turned and walked away, wanting to sulk. I turned back, before he got inside and I called out at him, 'My resistance is low.'

Mollie Quinn kept her lips sucked in as if she knew so many scandalous things she could tell would strike the whole countryside dumb should she let them out. Like a plague unleashed. But, of course, she would not tell because it was not her place to tell. Oh no. But if she wished . . . ! And Father Blackwell now, well! there you have it. Things! Oh yes, things! No sense of dignity there, for a start, if you *must* know. Always poking about in her kitchen where he had no business to be, God knows. And that's only the simplest thing. And Mollie Quinn would not mention such a thing as a priest's carrying on. That was not her business. No, that was God's business. *Carrying on!* She would not, she said, discuss Father's business with anyone, and she would not, she said, mention that strap Lil. Now Lil was the one female woman in Mollie Quinn's long years of service in the presbytery who would walk in the back door without as much as a by-your-leave, would fling some daft remark to Mollie (calling her Maggie, by the way), and breeze along through the hallway down to Father's room and go in without as much as a knock. Oh not a word. Not a word would pass Mollie's lips. No sir. And it happened like that time after time till Mollie began to wonder if she could ever unbuckle herself again around the bosom for ease and peace before the kneading of dough in case that strap would burst in upon her and discover her in a state of half-shame. Oh yes, she, poor Mollie, was atrociously put out. Trying to maintain her own position and integrity in her own kitchen, not asking anything out of life but the right to mind her own business and look after the welfare of those whose business it was to look after the welfare of the souls entrusted to their care. But she would, and she did, mention the day that two bishops, not one, but two, TWO, bishops, full bishops mind, TWO OF THEM, descended on the presbytery without warning and spent the whole of the afternoon inside in the parlour with Father Blackwell. Just as well the strap didn't stride in that particular afternoon, the overlarge hussy, God forgive me! Mollie was in a panic. There was a little drop of sherry in the house, cooking sherry. She had a swiss roll but one half of it was already gone. There were only two chocolate biscuits left in her special tin. Cooking sherry and half a swiss roll for TWO BISHOPS? She'd be disgraced throughout the whole of the Church militant. So she bundled herself into her outdoor clothes, shifted the kettle over onto the range and ran out the back door, hurrying as fast as her weight and her fur-lined boots would allow her, going the long way round to MacHenry's General Store in case the four eyes of two bishops should fall on her. She had an account with Mrs MacHenry and when she made it quite clear about the TWO bishops, she got her order made up very quickly indeed: a bottle of Irish whiskey, two chocolate swiss rolls, a packet of ginger snap biscuits, six slices of cooked ham and a fresh loaf. Mrs Mac herself drove her back to the presbytery the long way round so that she could ghost back into her kitchen with the goods. The kettle was lah-lahing. She opened the bottle of whiskey and poured a drop into an egg cup and swallowed it back, for two reasons, firstly to settle her own shattered nerves and secondly to make the bishops think that the whiskey bottle was already on hand and that a good housekeeper must be about. She wet a great pot of tea, and leaving it to draw on the hob, she brought the bottle of whiskey and two glasses on a tray (Father never takes whiskey in front of visitors – but behind their back! well! if she wanted to, couldn't Mollie say a word or two?); she straightened herself out and knocked quietly but firmly on Father's door; then without waiting for an answer, she went in. Well! Father Blackwell was sitting by the oval mahogany table in the bay window, gazing out on to the grey afternoon, his fingers drumming on the surface of the table. He was alone!

'Oh,' Mollie stuttered, 'I thought . . .' She stood inside the door, all her plans skittering on the floor about her feet.

'Oh the pukes, the pukes!' Father was muttering. And he sighed and half-turned to Mollie. 'They're gone, the sour oul' whures! And I'm shifted, Mollie, far side of the diocese, effective immediately. Oh the roarin' offensive whures and pukes!'

He got up suddenly and strode across the room and stood in
front of poor Mollie who thought he was going to strike her
for he looked as if he needed to strike someone or smash something but all he did was take the bottle off the tray and stand
there with it, hefting it, and then he said, 'I'm going out now
for a walk, Mollie, and I'll take a sup of the whiskey with me.'
And he breezed out of the room and out of the house.

Now when Mollie heard the shut of the hall door she took a
fine scoop out of the cooking sherry bottle and swallowed it
back, to help her recover from the shock and do you think
she didn't know where he was off to? Oh but she was soft,
Mollie, in her own way, and now he was being shifted out of
harm's reach it would be fair enough to give him a little spoiling, God help him, sure isn't he only human, too? and it would
be wrong to waste all the effort of the afternoon. And in the
evening sure wasn't the strap in the parlour with him. Lil! Oh
some Lily, that, some purity! A big bowler of a woman, as
bold as six brass fenders. Sitting up in the front bench at mass,
ogling up at him and her only a fly-by-night in the parish! The
Jezzy-ball! But in the evening when Mollie went in with the
tray and the cakes there she was in the big armchair and the
tears on her face and Father standing over her, hands behind
his back. Well, of course, Mollie said nothing, but left the tray
down quietly on the table instead of banging it down and
waded carefully through the thick silence and left them to
themselves. Bless them! Between you and me and the wall,
though, wasn't she some class of a Jezzy-ball, now?

'A fairy! a regular fairy! I used to call you that, way back then.'
    'Yes, I have a faint memory of that, Aunt Lil.'
    'No, dear, don't call me that, don't call me Lil. I was young

then, I had hopes, childish hopes. A childish name, Lil. Blackie used to call me *Lily* and I got to like the sound of the name in his mouth, it sounded more mature, somehow, more steady, Lily, makes you think life has been OK for you and now you can step into the middle of the road and walk along proudly.'

'Blackie? Do you mean Father Blackwell?'

'Yes, the old puke! Oh the puke! Do you know what? and only I'm a bit merry now on the gin I wouldn't be talking like this, even to you, dear. I loved him, the puke, I really and truly loved him. And what's more, I know for certain that he loved me. There now! what do you think of that?'

'It's not a surprise, Lily, I think we all knew it for a long time.'

'Maybe, maybe. And don't call me Lily, either! Not Lily! That name is too close to the heart. It hurts, now, to hear it. An Easter name. A spring name. Too pure a name, Lily. Pure and proud and virginal. And I had no ambitions to be virginal! No sir. No, not me. No ambitions in that direction at all at all. Pour me out another little bucketful of gin there, like a good fairy, and go gently on the tonic. Call me Lillian, there's a dear. Lillian. And sure you all knew about it, you knew he loved me, I think even that harridan Maggie-who's-it-his-bitch-of-a-housekeeper knew it but the only one that didn't know it was Blackie himself. A good priest, I reckon, but they don't know how to be good men, they don't know how to love. They can't get it right, none of them, pope nor bishop nor priest, they can't get it right, the relationship, I mean, between being a priest and being a man. Better still, forget the tonic. Give me the gin the way God made it, why go spoiling the work God sweated at by adding our own little fizzing negativities? Things were good between us, me and Blackie, I mean. Innocent, too. There was no hanky-panky, no such luck, but I was leading him up to it. Gradually. Poker games. Remember the poker games? Just a playful twiddle of my fingers on his wrist. A whist drive or two. An odd wink. Walks along the cliffs. Bumping shoulders between times. Oh good days, good days.'

'But he was a priest, Lillian, and those were tight times, weren't they?'

'*Lillian*, yes, nice to hear the word in your mouth, Henry. Lil-li-an. Dignified, slow, to go with my age, you know. God help me! But he won't, the old ba... Tight days they were indeed. Tight times. Eyes in hedges. Tongues like scythes. Minds like hoops. Soldered shut. But I had hopes, and he seemed to have hopes too. It wasn't unheard of, you know, even then. Priests, nuns, bishops, a pope or two, but I'd say it's a safe rule to steer clear of cardinals. There's something about cardinals that won't allow the female past. You never hear of a cardinal getting caught out with a woman... The rest of them, yes; maybe it's the scarlet, it is the cardinal hides in scarlet, amn't I right? Oh the pukes! didn't they descend on him like a pack of wolves on a limping lamb, the bishops, dozens of them landing on him, and they devoured all my days, all my nights, all my years!'

'Em, sorry, Lillian, if you'd like me to leave...'

'No, no, dear, no, it's good to see you. It's only the old gin that comes back out through my eyes. That's all. They have been lost days, all my days, lost, hadn't I fallen on God's good loving earth and didn't they pounce on me and turn my ground into daub with their bishops' shoes? Wasn't Blackie's flesh and soul torn into little shreds by them? laying down their laws without as much as a thought. As if love could be ordered and organised and put in its place, like a silken bookmark pressed tight between the pages of their black, fat missals! The pukes! Oh the hairy, unforgiven and unforgiving pukes! Here, Henry, another little gin there, love, it's a friend, you know, won't let you down ... We have a good relationship, gin and me, a good relationship. Just one more drop, dear Harry, em, Henry – or Tim? it was Tim, wasn't it? yes Tim, Tim-short-for-Timothy, that's right, just one more drop and don't be so afraid it'll shpill, even if it dosh shpill ... I'm just a wee bit tired now, dear, I'll nap, thanks for coming to shee me, you're the only one, you know, the only one in a long, long time ...'

A CLOSE ENCOUNTER

Leo was weary. Life, with its many disappointments, its punctures, its misaligned spokes, its buckled wheels, had brought him low. It would be a long, dispiriting haul on the bike over the roads to his father's house. It would take a great effort. To ready himself, to cross the yard, to haul the Rudge out from the shed, mount it, pedal . . . And Leo was weary. He would go – tomorrow? Even though he had promised . . . and a promise broken will be a ghost for life.

In the bewildering time between night and dawn Leo's father slipped out of life. An owl-soft departure. While all the watchers, who had succeeded through the deeps of darkness in remaining awake, finally yielded to the suggestion of coming light and had slept. The night-birds lessening the great wheeling of their flight. The eyes of the living growing moist with tiredness. Between times Leo's father ceased to be one thing and began to be something else.

When the phone rang in Leo's dream he came wide awake at once. As if he had been watchful in his sleep. He wore, even in bed, his many-coloured knitted dream-cap. It kept his thoughts under control and warmed the roots of his russet hair. It heated his dreams and kept his night-wanderings sensual and slow.

'Hah!'

'Leo?'

'Yup.'

'It's Kit.'

'Kit. It's you?'

''Tis.'

'Right!'

'Leo!'

'Yes.'

'Leo. I'm sorry.'

'Right.'

'No, but...'

'Yeah.'

'I'm sorry, Leo. This mornin'...'

'Right.'

'Leo...'

'Oh Kit. Kit. It's you!'

''Tis me, Leo. Sorry.'

'Not at all. How's things cuttin', Kit?'

'Fine, Leo, fine. Or, not really, it's just...'

'Right.'

'Leo. I'm sorry for yer thrubble...'

'Right.'

'If there's an'thin'...'

'Me thrubble?'

'I'm sorry for yer thrubble.'

'Daddy?'

'I'm sorry for yer thrubble.'

'Oh fuck it! No!'

'I'm very sorry, Leo . . .'

'Oh Chrisht! Oh no! Kit. 'Tis you, Kit, is in it?'

''Tis, Leo. I was there . . .'

'What time, Kit?'

'Musht a bin, let me see, 'bout six. This mornin'.'

'I'm comin' over, Kit.'

'Right. Leo, I'm sorry for yer thrubble.'

'Kit.'

Leo stood a long time. The sky was a thin, silver grey streak where the curtains didn't quite meet. He wore his pyjamas open at the shirt and crotch, dark blue pyjamas with lions regardant printed in a gentle orange. He stood so long, he was so thin, his pyjama bottoms fell of their own accord and piled themselves noiselessly about his ankles. He had promised his father, he had promised and sworn and now look! his father had gone and the promise had not been kept. Leo cursed himself for a didderer, a dodderer, a slack, his mind too often between two minds, between three or several minds. Now his father would hold him with an iron chain he could never break.

Leo wheeled his old Rudge out from the shed. He would have to face his father, and soon. It would be more difficult than ever now. He would have to kiss him, kiss that face that would be a cold, moist and accusing Otherthing. And if he did *not* kiss him, that would be a double hold his father would have over him for ever. A double chain he could not break. A broken promise *and* a withheld kiss! And if he *did* kiss him, would it not be a Judas kiss?

Leo ran his bike at the road and leaped up on it. It wobbled like a drunken foal, and Leo was off at speed down Hawthorn Lane, then a luscious back-wheel skidding turn down the Fuchsia Road. Leo on his bike was a many-coloured whirlwind, a gush, a squall, a happening. And then, suddenly, his heart failed within him and he knew he could not face his father alive or dead, his soul would shrivel up with the lie and become a worm squirming on the devil's hot palm.

The old Rudge had no brakes. Leo headed for the grassy margin that ran between the loose gravel surface of Sloe Road and the drain. The Rudge bucked and leaped and slithered, and slowed. Leo lifted a long leg off the pedal and let his boot work as a brake along the grass. He stopped. Hard by the edge of Woods's Wood. Silence attended his halting.

Leo lifted his bike over the raggedy barbed-wire fence of Woods's Wood and let it lean back against the wire. He gazed into the dark brown dimness of the wood where all the boles of the trees rose in their ordered ranks. There was a kind soughing from the pine needles and branches up above, God leaning down out of his heaven and breathing heavily with the effort, God's brown and dark-haired chest ready to welcome Leo and cool his fevered mind.

Leo held his trousers tight up under his crotch and hoisted one long leg over the barbed wire.

'The future of mankind may be in jeopardy,' he told his bike.

For a moment he stood astride the fence, halfway between the light of his duty and the darkness of his skulking. The mad notion of penance came to him; should he sit on the fence and barb himself? would his father be placated by Leo's lacerated testicles, by a pattern of rips in the flesh of his arse?

'Our Father, who art in heaven,' Leo said aloud.

Quickly then, before the foolishness of his soul got the better of him, he hoisted the other leg and placed himself inside the fence, out of harm's way. He hefted the Rudge and wheeled it in over the soft ground that was a layering of the droppings of centuries: leaf and pine-needle, branch and bole, nest and bird-shit, vole and mole and badger-bone, the

vomiting of owl and the leavings of many a secretive lover. A
darkness fragrant and soothing.

He found a rich-leafed sycamore in the stomach-area of the
wood. He propped the bike against the bole of the tree, stood
on a pedal, then on the cross-bar and reached to the first branch
high over his head. As he kicked himself up the bike heeled
over slowly and fell with a patient sigh of wheel-spokes and
chain-rust and left Leo dangling like a wet rope from the
branch. He swung his legs and had the tree in a scissors-grip,
then hoisted himself, nimbly enough, considering, up into the
mothering arms of the tree. He climbed. Little branches fell,
his boots scraped the bole of the tree and small drops of resin-
blood were shed. He climbed higher until his head, with the
many-coloured dream-cap, emerged over the trees like an
exotic bird appearing over the green heaving of an ordinary
ocean.

Leo swayed gently with the gentle swaying of the tree. His
breath returned to him like a flock of starlings settling in the
woods at night. The breezes cooled him. The grey sky re-
assured him. His thoughts settled. He began to wonder. His
body urged itself against the body of the tree. His father had
not liked him to look at girls. But he had looked at girls.
And he had imagined girls. Big ones. More beautiful and
daring than any of the local girls, who giggled behind their
hands in the chapel pews. He had imagined his many-coloured
dream-cap waving in the air like a victorious flag while his
long body was eased of its length between the . . . He stopped
himself.

'Mammy,' he said aloud.

A heron came flapping along the pavement of the air like an
old sick man in dressing gown and slippers. It saw the many-
coloured dream-cap, squawked and hit some barrier in the air;
it tried to turn but flopped heavily down against the tips of the

trees, where it battled a while before rising again and flying away at an angle towards the furthest limits of Woods's Wood. Its dignity wounded. Its long legs folded back. Leo sniffed.

'We are bound by unreal chains,' he called after the heron.

He imagined himself standing on the very tip of the sycamore, raising his long arms and soaring away in perfect detachment from the demands of the world. The demands of his body. He sniffed again. A man grows foolish...

Perhaps if he did not take the direct route to his father's house? Perhaps, he thought, he could *sidle* there. Pretend he was going somewhere else. Go the long way round. Walk. He did not need to give his attention to what he had to do. He could fool himself. Take himself unawares. Express surprise that he had hit upon his father's house. Then he could sidle through the gawking, smirking throng, Kit and Packie and Nobby and Floyd, Judy and Julie and Sheila and Joan, he could nod at them, hand them out small words of greeting like cough lozenges from his small tin box. Knock up against his father's coffin and inadvertently touch his lips to that stone forehead. The reality of the world is a chain bound about the flesh of a man.

Leo climbed down from his perch. He was a long, gliding, snake. For a moment he had to hang out from the branch over emptiness since the bike had fallen away from under him. He was scared to let go. He waited. Soon his arms began to grow stiff and sore, his fingers slip on the branch. He let go then. He had to. He curled up on the earth, glad that decisions were being made for him.

He left the bike tethered to the sycamore and set off, wandering slowly through the fragrant, liminal world of the wood. Tall as an alder. Flitting. He paused at the edge of Woods's Wood, peering out like a night-animal on the day.

There were fields to cross. A townland. More fields. Then his father's house. He hoisted himself again, one hand hefting his crotch out of risk's way, and stood astride the barbed-wire fence for a while, one foot in darkness, one in light. Then he came to Borders' River, more stream than river, gathering up the drainage from the fields and meadows and carrying it down towards the larger rivers. There was a crossing a little to his right, a few railway sleepers laid down and covered with mosses, lichens and the lives that live between lives. Leo took it, cautiously; it was treacherous, slimy, slippery. He stood on the planks and listened to the easy gurgling of the water under him. His eyes glazed over. His hand remained still against his crotch. He stared into the hollow shell of himself.

When he reached his father's house the afternoon had advanced. Leo opened the back door into the kitchen. Kit was sitting inside the door, squat as a stone god carved from the early ages of mankind. Others sat about the table, in corners, on stools, on the old horse-hair sofa. A low murmur of conversation died as Leo came in. He raised his hand in greeting. Kit looked up, a bottle of stout in his hand.

'Leo!'

'Kit.'

''S upstairs.'

'K.'

'Took yer time.'

'Thrubble with th' oul bike. Ya know.'

'Yeah. Thrubble.'

Leo moved quickly to the door into the hallway. He climbed the stairs slowly and entered his father's room. Mrs Hansberry from the town was sitting at the foot of the bed. Watching. Keeping the corpse company.

'Leo,' she whispered. 'Sorry for yer thrubble.'

'Thanks, Mrs Hansb'y.'

She lifted her shapeless black presence from the chair and shambled out of the room. There was an unbearable silence when she closed the door behind her. Leo's father lay, dressed in his Sunday and market suit, best shirt, best tie. There was a shine to his shoes there never had been before. The bed was flawless. The pillow scarcely dunted by the old demanding head. The jaw was bandaged, from chin to crown, to keep the mouth from falling open. Just as well, for Leo expected words of remonstration, admonitory mumblings. The hands were joined about the black berries of a rosary.

'Daddy.'

Leo stood at a safe distance. A single candle burned at the bedside, near a small brass crucifix and a drinking glass of blessed water. Leo imagined he could hear the heavy breathing of the candle.

'I'm sorry, Daddy.'

The words sounded all wrong in the emptiness. Like a candle guttering in bright sunshine. Like a curse in the mouth of a young nun.

'Daddy. Please?'

Leo was whispering now. He took off his many-coloured dream-cap and moved forward hesitantly.

'Let me go. I'm sorry I'm late comin'. Not today. I don't mean today. I mean before. My promise. I tried. I really did.'

Leo bent his long body forward, the dream-cap crushed in his hands. Pleading. The body lay stiff and silent as a log. And as alien. Leo looked up at the iron frame at the head of the bed. There were little flecks of rust on it. Then he lunged his long head down and kissed his father quickly on the clamped-together lips. Leo was too tall for such a movement; he lost his balance and his body fell over that of his father, left hand

clutching at the old white head for support. The bandage fell
loose from about the head. The mouth opened slowly and a
long exhalation, like a sigh, was released. There was a cave of
darkness within. Leo's mouth fell open too. He turned quickly
and went to the door. Mrs Hansberry was outside, her head
too close to the door, and she jerked back when Leo opened it
so suddenly, her face, the colour of wet cement, flushed a sickly
damson hue.

'Ah,' Leo said. 'His, ah, his, ah, thing came off. He, ah,
opened his mouth like. You might, ah, fix it? Mrs Hansb'y?
Please?'

Mrs Hansberry's mouth fell open, too. Was she to be witness, or near witness, to a miracle?

Leo went rapidly down the stairs and out the front door as
quickly as his long legs would take him. He put on his many-
coloured dream-cap and set out for Looney's, just a half-mile
down the road. He needed to be consoled by quietness. And
stout. For a while. To tie himself back together again. In his
own world. The real world. Leo's world.

It was dusk, the in-between time of day, when Leo came again
to the planks laid across Borders' River. His whole body was
lolling now with loss and stout. He walked on the soft grass
verges of the roads and laneways, now on the right-hand side,
now on the left. He made his way along meadows, following
the contours of their hedges and fences. At times a cow in a
field seemed to separate from herself and stand, full cow half
cow, before his vision. He wondered where he had left his old
Rudge.

There was a young woman standing on the other side of
Borders' River, just across the sleepers. *Sexy*, was the word
that sprang to Leo's mind. And *Sorry, Daddy*, followed

instantly, like a pain. She was tall and full-bodied, the stuff of Leo's waking dreams, her long straw-coloured hair was beautifully unkempt about her lovely face; her lips were pouting berry-red, a poppy in a field of sedge; her eyes, as far as he could tell, were grey-blue-green; she wore a black leather jacket glistering with silver studs, silver zips and badges; decisive red boots came to just below her knees, a red leather skirt that gleamed reached from below her navel to well above those knees; a tiny red tank-top left her midriff exposed and her full breasts peered out from the top at Leo through the dusk. Around her neck hung several brass chains, hammered nails on the ends of them, a big, brass crucifix.

Leo gulped. She was smiling at him. She stood there languidly, as if waiting just for him. She shifted a little where she stood and he could hear the crinkling of her leathers and the clinking of her brasses. She started to hum softly, as if to herself, a tuneless, cooing, wordless song.

'Thought you'd be in white,' Leo said from his side of the drain.

'White's out,' she said; 'pisses me off.' Her voice resinous and low, chuckling like the waters of the stream.

'Thought you'd be old an' wrinkled an' ugly.'

She laughed. 'Shows how you get conned by what they say.'

'Thought you'd be shriekin' an' screamin' an' keenin' an' combin' out your long white hair.'

'No subtlety in the screaming, Leo,' she said, 'that's all old hat. And there's such a thing as hairsprays now, you know.'

'Anyway,' Leo said triumphantly, 'you're late! You should 'a bin here last night!'

.'That depends on how you decide on things, Leo. Time's a chain, a rosary, and you can go round and round it till you're dizzy. Who's to say that now is not last evening or last evening isn't now? It's up to you, you know, Leo, it's up to you.'

Leo wished he were younger, more sober, more *au fait* with the ways of the young ones, more – with it. She was piercingly attractive, that lovely face, those breasts, that navel, those legs, she was a vision against the soft greens and warm browns of the dusky edge of Woods's Wood. Leo was without words. His body trembled with wishes. His many-coloured dream-cap quivered.

'Come on over,' the beautiful woman beckoned to him.

She was taking off her black leather jacket. The chains about her neck and midriff sounded like a sacramental tinkling of bells. Leo shook his head, the way you'd shake the raindrops off an umbrella. The woman turned away, stooped, laid her jacket over the barbed-wire fence. Her buttocks, under the red leather mini-skirt, were a feast, a festival, an invitation. She turned her lovely head and smiled at Leo over her shoulder. Her hands moved to undo the chain about her waist. He grunted and stepped onto the wooden planks over the drain.

Leo was weary. Life, with its many disappointments, its punctures, its misaligned spokes, its buckled wheels, had brought him low. It would be a long, dispiriting haul on the bike over the roads to his father's house. It would take a great effort. To haul the Rudge out from the shed, mount it, pedal, pedal, pedal... And Leo was weary. He would go – tomorrow? Even though he had promised... and a promise broken will be a ghost for life. He made a supreme effort and lifted himself with a groan out of the bed. His father, after all, was his father and a promise made was a promise made.

LAWRENCE

There's a thing.
?
A terrible thing.
Go on. Say it, why don't you?
Shocking, so it is.
Say it.
D.H. Lawrence!
D.H. Lawrence?
Frightful.
You think so?
I know it. My God! *Lady Chatterly's Lover*. My God! And
another thing . . .
Yeah?
Desperate, truly, frightfully awful.
What?
Joyce!
Joyce?
Joyce.
He's Irish. Dublin.
Makes it worse. That criminal *Ulysses*.
Criminal?
That disgusting Milo O'Shea.

What about him?

In *Ulysses*.

There's no Milo O'Shea in *Ulysses*.

In the film. Disgusting.

What?

There's that . . . you know.

What?

Well. I'm sure you don't even know the word.

What word?

Masturbation.

Masturbation?

I bet you don't even know what it means.

(. . .)

It just goes to show . . .

What?

That Joyce was a terrible villain.

And D.H. Lawrence?

Yes, and a lot more.

(. . .)

What will you be studying?

English. English literature.

I knew it. Anything to upset me.

(. . .)

I burned it, you know.

What?

Picked it up with the tongs and dropped it on the fire.

What?

That Rodney Doyle's filth.

What? *The Commitments?*

I found it in your room. Some bedside-reading that. Every second word a swear word.

You went into my room, appropriated my book and burned it?

It's for your own good.

He's not even on the course.

You could study Francis Thompson, Joseph Mary Plunkett, Pearse. 'I fled Him, down the nights and down the days.' And what about that lovely poem, what is it again? something about the mother, and seeing her two strong sons go out...

But that's war.

There you are, you see?

See what?

Godless, full of sex and cursing, and running down your own patriot dead, that's what you want, that's all there is nowadays. And I'm proud of it, of burning that book, and Lawrence, too, I burned that book, what was it? *Women in Love*. Disgusting! And Joyce, I burned that. Literature! Psah! I don't know what the young generation is coming to at all, I just don't know. Values. That's it. No values. Nothing to hold on to. And you talk about writing. Now when I was young...

THE SINS OF THE FATHERS

Mossy Goggins's first strong memory was of a day he looked in the cracked and bandage-repaired bathroom mirror. His father had just finished shaving; the long, mean razor was back on the wooden shelf, the shaving brush, like the cut-off tail of a baby squirrel, stood beside it; in the basin a rim of off-white foam lurked dirtily. Mossy faced himself in the mirror and saw his father looking back out at him, red eyes rounded with a brown scum of age and pain, porridge-grey face lined and ruffled, a caved-in jaw and purple veins outlining deltas of sin and misery all over his cheeks and forehead. And behind him again, or in front of him, his mother stood at the bathroom door, gazing in, grinning an awful grin from a black, toothless mouth. He looked round quickly. There was nobody behind him. When he looked back into the mirror he saw only himself again, a small, healthy face, eyes bright, skin still smooth and touchable as a baby's arse.

Mossy heard noises. Noises all over the house, floorboard-and-rafter noises he interpreted as the steppings of Lucifer creatures. Scratchings and blunderings along the wainscottings and eaves. He would open his eyes as widely as possible in the darkness of his bedroom, straining for vision. He would get out of bed, waiting for those clammy, seaweed-wet hands to clutch him, he would make his way like a blundering moth to his parents' room, knock timidly out of his darkness, open the door and be scolded and fatherhandled back to his bed.

Now he was sitting in his wheelchair looking down from the cliff-top over the sea. A school of porpoises gambolled across the bay. Out of nowhere came the question: *Did the porpoises create the sunshine or did the sunshine create the porpoises?* Like one of those echoes of nonexistent voices he had heard when he was young. 'Who gives a . . . !' he snorted aloud, but the words seemed to hang on the air, a putrid stench about them, and he let them drop. The long grey bodies curved out of the water, curved back down again, silently, as if the sea were doodling them, shaping circles and half-circles out of its own being, writing perfectly rhymed couplets of poetry and as quickly erasing them.

Mossy Goggins settled the rug about his limbs and scowled out at the Atlantic. He had thought of a phrase that was certain to cut through his father's soul like a slash-hook. He would fling it at him, when the proper moment came, in the evening, after he had settled by the TV for the news:

I will never forgive your God for my existence!

Then, without waiting for a reply – and what reply could there be? – he would wheel himself noisily over the linoleum floor and out the door to his own room. That word *your* was good, it spread the blame, and blamed his father, without saying it in so many words. It was a phrase that would stay in his father's soul like a long line with multiple hooks dropped into the sea.

On hardy evenings of storm, The Gunner Floyd used to step in out of his own dank loneliness and take a place by the Goggins's hearth, the old people murmuring nonsense, yarns, incantations, charms. 'If you lave narry a gift on the offering tables of the dead,' he pronounced, 'they'll be back to you, quick as shite, you mark my words now, making you pay with your offerings of fear, over and over and over.'

The Gunner's yarns were garnished with years of porter, peppered with half-memories of falling into drains and bog-holes when his eyes were yellow with the light of intoxication and wolves with the heads of gravediggers stalked the alder hedgerows of his near-neglected land. But Mossy would sit, under the shadows of his father and mother, his mouth falling open with the weight of his credulity.

'The divil his-self has left his mark beyant on the road from Darby's lane to the graveyard; a hoofprint big as the acreage of a fat man's arse and rain nor wind nor 'lectric storm will not shift it. Prowls the land, he do, looking for sweet, virginal flesh to suck.'

'Now, now, Floyd,' Mossy's father would say, 'keep any suggestions of – you know, *that!* – out of it. Remember, there's a young boy here, a young boy.'

Mossy's flesh had been sweet then, he sat safe within the circle of the elders. Those nights of storm the walls of the house were rebuilt by the devil and his angels, by cackling goblins and gobbling cacklers cursed by God to roam the earth and find those fattened for their tables by banquets of sin. The fallen and the falling angels, flung out of God's stable-yard for grovelling in the muck of their own pride, caught now between worlds where all they had to do was gnaw at the sacred lives of those not yet doomed to eternal misery.

On the cliff-top, the brakes of his wheelchair applied, Mossy Goggins remembered. And cursed. His mother. His father. Gunner Floyd. Himself. The world.

He had grown big; at least the upper half of him was big, muscular, his face like the bole of a thorn-tree, grey and rugged and stiff. The muscles in his chest and arms and shoulders were powerful. Mossy wheeled himself up and down the road from his house to the sea, over and over and over again at a speed and ferocity that ought to have burned all anger and viciousness out of his soul. But the lower half of his body was a shame, as if the roots of his life were cankered and the flowering of his days must quickly perish. Today was one of those days when whole families would be gathering to the beaches, where they would strut in near nakedness on the sand and in the shallows, playing the old familial games, or acting out the sexual charade. Oh how he hated them all, especially the women, whose tall, lovely bodies hurt his stomach with longing, but whose eyes held for him only that strained grey of pity and embarrassment.

I will never forgive your God for my existence.

'Every man,' said The Gunner Floyd, 'every man is brang into this world with his own shadow, a shadow and a ghost and the shadow of a ghost. And for every man the day will come, some certain day, soon or late, when a man will meet his own shadow and the ghost of his own shadow face to face. And that, may the Holy Mother of Jesus Christ protect us, will be that!'

Mossy was sent, each evening, for milk, down the hilly road, over the gate into Harte's meadows, across the bottoms where one slowly rotting plank leaned over an unthinkable world of spawning frogs and bottomless muck, and up the creaking lane into the yard of Tessa Mulcrone's old house. Tessa had lived alone for centuries, and centuries ago her husband had died, and she had lived on and on and on, harvesting all the words of ill-luck and catechetical ghost-mongering that she could find. Mossy Goggins panted with fear before the door of her house. There was a comforting, butter yellow glow from the small window to the right of the door. Behind him was the swaying ocean of darkness, with its lobster-reaching horrors, its octopuses of terror, its lechering and squelching, sidling figures of woe.

'You look like you've been to see the devil himself and met yourself coming back,' Tessa would tell him. She was always muttering while she managed herself about, filling his can out of her churn, grinning at him with her empty red mouth, light behind her and the certainty of a turf fire. 'You're a grand boy, Mossy,' she whined, 'a grand boy, the spitting image of your father, God help us, the very eyes, the same bones, the same mouth. An' all, an' all . . .'

Mossy always ran back, ran and ran and ran, small spillings of milk spattering the world behind him as darkness followed with its load of distress.

'Did you pass yourself out yet, young Mossy Goggins?' asked The Gunner Floyd. And Mossy hated them all, he hated his father, he hated his mother, he hated The Gunner Floyd though he did not know it yet, hated them for planting such seeds of terror in his freshly raked soil.

Mossy's father, Lukey, was an ashplant in a waistcoat and galluses. Mossy's mother, Madge, was a parsnip wrapped in a florid apron. Mossy's life at home was a life of plodding and ploughing, his bones were strengthened by carrying heavy burdens from field to haggard and from stable to meadow, his feet were heavy from stomping about in plosh. His fingers grew fat and hard, his nails were black, his hands were sensitive as shovels. But the ghosts began to withdraw into the whitewashed walls as he grew older and realised that he had escaped, so far, all evil things. Mossy went to bed so wearily each night that ghosts and walking shadows grew weary of their efforts to rouse him.

Until the day he was forking hay from the cart to the loft. Prod and prod, hoist, pitch, withdraw. Prod and prod, hoist, pitch, withdraw. Time after time. His thoughts, if you could call them thoughts, moving on young Dolores Fadian who lived in town, in the small and protected row of houses known as Yellow Crescent; he thought how she looked in jeans and jumper, how her body crowed when she bent to gather up the shakings or go guggering down the ridges. Oh how he would like to prod, and prod, hoist, pitch and withdraw there. Sure enough. Rightly.

He stopped himself, then. That was a sin, his father would have said, it was a sin even to think like that. A sin, to think of Dolores Fadian's arse. Even the word *arse* was a sin in itself. And his soul, his pale immortal soul, was in peril of becoming porridge on Satan's breakfast table.

Mossy Goggins saw a shadow fall across the wall of hay before him. There was no sunshine coming from behind. There was scarcely ever sunshine. There was rain and slow mists and lurching caravels of fog. But there was his shadow! Shifting when he shifted, prodding, hoisting, pitching, withdrawing. But each time the shadow seemed to grow in size and menace, seemed to swell and loom over Mossy Goggins where he worked. Mossy began to sweat. He speared the hayfork into the wall of hay and hurried away from the spot.

When he came in the house he found his mother dead. Just like that. Just, dead. Having swallowed down her shadows and the ghost of her shadow and the shadow of her ghost. In one gulp. Dead. His mother, still in her florid apron, sitting in her usual chair in front of the fire. The fire, too, was dead. She had her arms folded in her lap in a gesture of complete resignation. Or expectation. Her head lay forward over her breasts. Parsnip-breasts. Long-dried. She seemed at first to be merely dozing, waiting perhaps for a soda-cake to swell to perfection in the oven.

When he came into the kitchen Mossy began talking to her at once, telling her about the shadow that had risen before him where there was no sunshine. He knew it wouldn't mean much to her but the silence he got back from her was unacceptable. He shook her, gently, to wake her, but she merely toppled sideways, slowly, stiffly, and met her own thin shadow on the floor. Mossy screamed. He called his father. There was no response. He ran out the back door, shouting, then he ran in again and ran upstairs to try and find him.

He found him. On the bed, one with his long shadow, his galluses strained to bursting over his long-stretched-out body, his hands folded neatly over his chest. He was fully dressed, as if he had lain himself down on the covers of the bed to catch a few winks before the demands of the evening. He had his boots on. There were small wisps of straw and little brown sods of cowdung on the boots. Mossy thought, at first, he was dead. Then he got the overwhelming acid smell of the drink. His father snorted like a great horse. And Mossy wished he had found him dead too. He tried to break the news of downstairs gently but all he got for answer was another snort and a great whiff of sour whiskey.

The funeral mass was a sad one, Lukey Goggins moving in his guilt like a dead thing. There and not there. At the appropriate time Mossy went up to stand beside the priest and view the neighbours, relations and friends as they dropped their offerings into the baskets left on the coffin top. He stood, adult, his hands redly folded over his crotch, assessing the state of affairs. He was the centre of a great sunshine of sympathy and understanding and the one pound coins, and even three five-pound notes, were ostentatiously placed in the basket as he watched. He nodded, morosely, to his acquaintances. Finally, when all had done, he reached deep into his trouser pockets for his own offering. His pockets were empty! This was his new suit, his funeral suit. He had forgotten to transfer his money . . .

For a few moments he fidgeted before the priest and the watchful eyes of the congregation; he sniffed loudly, used his handkerchief, fumbled and reached from pocket to pocket. He knew he was growing red as a turnip. His father, lost in whatever thoughts were left him, kept his head down over the pew. What could Mossy do? he was lost. He would be a talking-point for ever in every reach and tuck of the townland. He turned his back on priest and congregation, he turned his back on father and coffin, he went down, head low, to his place.

'If you lave narry a gift on the offering tables of the dead, they'll be back to you, quick as shite . . .'

Lukey Goggins was sitting in the lounge of the Westport Hotel. It was his day to take his own father, Luke, Luke Goggins senior, to lunch in the hotel. Luke had been a big man, once. Now he had shrunk till he looked like a dried mangel.

'Would you like dessert, Father?' Lukey asked. The old man shook his head and went on masticating his chop.

'I'll go and get me some jelly and custard,' Lukey said, unwinding himself from the cane chair and heading back to the buffet in the lounge. There was only one other person about at this hour of the afternoon, a priest, dozing over a newspaper in a corner. Lukey wanted it that way, because his father, Luke . . . well, Lukey had been carrying Luke on his shoulders for so many years. He was growing heavier by the week.

Every Wednesday, for the last decade, Lukey drove his tractor up the long arterial road into the hills. Seven miles out, he turned right, up a lane at the end of which was the family home where his father stubbornly continued to live. The lane was pitted, pocked and rutted; trees as ancient as the old man leaned in and down, cluttering and darkening the lane, keeping it permanently wet and dripping.

At the end of the world, between fertile earth and barren mountain rock, Luke Matthew Goggins insisted on scraping at his few acres. His ground was gritty and mean; rushes, ferns, furze bushes a standing army of ragamuffin youths threatening to overrun him. Old Luke kept two cows, an ass, a few hens. But all his land was filled with snipe, skylark, fox, hare, undisturbed by him, guarded, courted, loved. The yard about the mountain house was a shallow pool of manure and chickenshit that sometimes dried into a thin scab. The fields lost space every year to sallies and brambles; the corner of each field, churned into mud by the ass and cows, got wetter and wetter. Lukey itched to get at the place but old Luke held on to life by his fingernails. Somewhere, deep down in the dark cellars of his own life, Lukey wished that the grip would loosen and the man would fall.

Lukey waited at the register for his change. He had his pint of milk during lunch while his father slobbered over a glass of Guinness. Lukey eyed the rows of bottles behind the bar; he had chucked all that, years ago, after that dreadful day. He leaned back and looked at the old man. He watched him chew, the base of the chin rising almost to the nostrils, little dribbles down the chin, the gravelly satisfaction on the old face. Lukey shivered with a sudden cold. What a weight! what a burden! well-nigh intolerable, and unavoidable.

Up on the cliff ledge Mossy sat, gazing listlessly over the sea. His anger and frustration had wearied him and he settled back in his chair in a kind of stillness. He saw the long, evaporating trail of an aeroplane high in the sky above him, flying west, out over the sea, slicing through the thin, radiant air. He said the names out loud, *Acapulco, Las Vegas, Florida*, imagining the laughter, the cocktails, the lovely women parading by with thongs to emphasise their nakedness, the men, body builders, all slow-motion rippling of muscles, the men and women all preening themselves under a generous sun, their slow and choreographed ballet denied for ever to a clump like him.

Yet he had had hopes, even after his mother's death. As soon as he thought it acceptable for him to do so, Mossy had allowed the image of bosomy, full-arsed, sturdy-thighed Dolores Fadian to shimmy in his mind. If he could take her as his missus, perhaps he could persuade his father to knock down the old brown tainted house and build a new one? or perhaps Grandfather Luke would soon drift away and Mossy could have the mountain farm?

Mossy Goggins was not an appropriate name for the courting life. Maurice. That was better. Maurice Mark Goggins. He would impress himself, and others, with that. He would impress Dolores. So Maurice Mark Goggins went to town and was astonished how quickly and unblushingly the delectably fleshed Dolores agreed to his stuttering and unasked question. He would allow a suitable delay, a hiatus. Soon he would marry and the world would be at his feet. He tried hard to avoid thinking of . . . her *bum*, her breasts, her . . . flesh.

Then he made his mistake. One morning Maurice Mark Goggins took the brown towel away from before the old mirror in the bathroom and began to shave himself. He picked up his father's old razor, long and mean and sharp. He used his father's old shaving brush, like the cut-off tail of a baby squirrel; in the basin a rim of off-white foam lurked dirtily. His face buried in lather, he gazed deep into the mirror's soul. And there, as once before, his father's face stared back at him, red eyes rounded with a brown scum of age and pain, porridge-grey face lined and ruffled, a caved-in jaw and purple veins outlining deltas of sin and misery all over his cheeks and forehead. And behind him his grandfather's face, blanched by age? or by anger at the thoughts that coursed through Mossy's evil brain? Maurice Mark Goggins closed his eyes. Shamed. Conscious of sin.

He opened them again. There was a small, healthy face, eyes bright, skin still smooth and touchable as a baby's arse, staring back out at him. He turned and fled from the old bathroom, fled so quickly that his foot caught on the torn carpet on the landing and he went tumbling and cartwheeling down the stairs. He remembered, when he came to himself in the hospital, seeing his own whirling, flailing shadow come up those awful stairs to meet him. And just before his eyes closed he could see Dolores Fadian, endowed Dolores Fadian, and she was standing in his barn, feet firmly planted and wide apart, her generous, hay-hued body was wholly naked, and her hands reached out to him, beckoning him, beckoning...

On his cliff Mossy Goggins had slipped into an uneasy sleep, sitting self-pityingly in his wheelchair. For a while all the ghosts he had known came and salivated through his dream, his mother, The Gunner Floyd and Tessa Mulcrone, and there, too, came Dolores, her lovely flesh suntanned and smooth. He woke suddenly. In a rage of sweat. The wheelchair moved. It was slipping towards the cliff's edge and, waking into nightmare, Mossy felt himself fall slowly out onto the mercies of the air, so slowly that he scarcely believed it was happening. For a moment it seemed as if he was seated on a column of air, the sea surging as usual far beneath him and breaking on the black rocks. The chair dropped slowly, like a feather almost, the wheels still turning gently. Then it struck an outcrop of rock

and spun, sickeningly. Mossy screamed and flung his arms
wildly. His fingers scrabbled against loose clay on the top of
the cliff and his elbow struck fiercely against rock. Then his
right hand closed about something and he felt his body jerked
out of its fall and slapped back against the face of the cliff. He
was hurt, and winded, but he had stopped his fall. He reached
his left hand and clasped the stump of a tree-root in the soil, a
small fuchsia root that had been growing there before the ero-
sion of the cliff. It held.

Mossy heard the crash of the wheelchair against the rocks
below. His head was in between his arms; he could not look
down. He clung fiercely, with both hands. He was strong.
The muscles on his shoulders, arms and wrists were powerful.
He could hold on. He tried to hoist himself up a little but his
nether body dragged against the cliff and he could not rise. He
screamed: *Help!* The scream flew like a hawk high up over the
cliff-top, hovered there a while, then disappeared into the
warm air above.

His upper arms were hurting. There was sweat on his forehead. He clenched his teeth, hard. He looked up and saw the
glorious purity of the sky, without a trace of cloud. He did
not want to die. He thought of the chair beside the fire on a
wet evening, how he relished the comfort of his home, the
gentle ticking of the turf as it collapsed in the grate...

'Our Father,' he began, whispering the words, 'Our Father,
who art in heaven...'

He knew that, when he fell, at least the lower half of his
body would know no pain, it would be paper, crumbling.
He heard the remote drone of an aeroplane. He looked up
and saw the white thread move across the sky. He wondered,
idly, about its passengers, he did not envy them now. Not the
surf, and the sex, and the dance-floors. He envied them life.
That was all. Life, the great flower of their living that bloomed

and opened out in their lives – that he envied.

And then, as if he had fallen back into a dream, he saw his father's face appear between him and the sky, he saw his father's hand reach down to him out of nowhere, he heard his father's voice speak out his name: 'Mossy, Mossy!', urgently, with caring, and concern, and he closed his eyes in joy and breathed a long, deep sigh of gratitude.

CAPITAL H

There are cliffs that stand tall and immaculate, facing from the island westward on to empty ocean. The gannets come from far out, soar, and dive into the sea by these cliffs. Occasionally the great, slow, hulk of a basking shark cruises close to the rocks below. On warmer days, schools of porpoises go by in rhythmic, delirious ballet movements. On wild days the whole Atlantic Ocean comes to throw itself against the cliffs and then the world darkens, the cliff birds wrap themselves into themselves and press their bodies into crevices for shelter. When the world stills again, and the sun appears and shadows the cliff ledges with their pink flowers and their heathers, the detritus of human living can be seen in these remote coves, floating like scum on the heaving surface or lodged like graffiti among the rocks: cans, boxes, plastic bags, and wheels.

Popsy Foran climbed down sometimes to the very edge of the sea and came back with tyres, buckled bicycle wheels, pram wheels, even steering wheels. These he placed around his demountable, growing flowers in those that were large enough to contain the earth, making shapes of the bicycle and pram wheels, propping cartwheels up against his fence and painting them with the colours of his childhood. Redeeming them.

It was Sunday morning. Quite a normal Sunday morning. A few swarms of raindrops had flown by but now the sun was shining, feebly. The first bell had sounded. There was a chill breeze that threatened more serious rain before the day was over. Otherwise there was the usual emptiness on the island roads: cars and tractors dozing in their places, their wheels still. In many houses rashers and eggs had been fried and the luscious scents had wafted out to aggravate the cats and dogs that lounged about the little yards. Now the people donned their Sunday bests, they polished their shoes, they unknotted last Sunday's ties, put them around their necks, knotted them again.

Popsy got up early. It was, he knew, an ordinary day, the thirteenth Sunday in ordinary time, in an ordinary world. And there was ordinary light about the day, ordinary, every-day scuffling between sunshine and rain, between breeze and calm. He opened the door of his demountable and stepped out into the day. If Popsy had been a travelling man, his de-mountable would have been a caravan mounted on four magnificent wheels. He would have painted it all the colours of the sacred serpents and fitted it out with a chimney stack that would end high in the sky like the torn lid of a badly opened can. And there would be horses, high-stepping, shaggy-maned horses, ready to draw Popsy on his way around the curves and corners of the spinning world.

'That's not the way it's to be, though, is it,' he said out loud, saying the words to the fence, saying them contentedly, expecting no answer, not this time, because it wasn't a question, it was a statement.

Sometimes the noises in Popsy's head were like an over-flowing cistern, water running freely where it must not run, in a slow and ineluctable swelling. And sometimes the sounds within his head were dry sounds, the sounds a small army of

insects would make as they chewed and legged their way inside the petals of a dahlia. He did not greatly worry about such
noises. He could sit very still, close his eyes gently, and wait for
them to fade away. Like a crowd going off arguing over the
county game. He was more anxious when his eyesight
dimmed, when the world grew fuzzy about him, in a snowstorm of black and white dancing spots, the way the television
screen often went. He imagined it happening when he was
wheeling his barrow onto the main road, or his bicycle down
Main Street. But then he would shake his head, as if to fling
away raindrops, and remember that there was a guiding hand,
a kindly palm that held him in its hollow, to see him home, to
lift him out of thorny ways.

'What was it He said?' (Even in Popsy's unformed thoughts
the H was a capital H.) 'Something like do not fear, o ye of
little faith, for not even a sparrow falls to the ground, or lifts a
foot against a stone, but even the hairs of your head are num-
bered and . . . something else, too. Like that. He said. So.'

Popsy spoke to himself a good deal. And to Himself. Popsy
took for text all that they had taught him down the years. For
text, for truth. Laying his life down on His hands, on that
kindly palm, while the wheel turned. Laying himself down
to sleep on the floor of his demountable for didn't He say that
foxes have holes but He had nowhere to lay down His head?

The council had allocated his fried-sausage-brown demountable to Popsy several years ago, when he was proven harmless.
It had been set up on a small plot of land, several blankets large.
It was mounted on bricks to keep the lightweight wooden
building from soaring off with the skylarks. And it was further
held to the earth by a series of ropes flung across it and fixed
round the concrete blocks. Like overturned boats. At the
round ocean's edge. He grew daffodils, irises, tulips, roses,
cornflowers, lupins, gladioli. In wheels. In old black iron pots,

pots coveted by the collectors. Popsy's hands, chipped, chapped and calloused, could coax a sunflower to bloom in darkness.

They had given him a wheelbarrow and a shovel. He went where there were works in progress. He went on his bicycle. He loaded the wheelbarrow with grit and followed the works, filling in the awkward angles, levelling off the edges, filling holes. He lived as if the other workers didn't see him. They left him alone. They never teased him. They knew he was in God's care.

Popsy stepped down from his demountable and touched the earth. He could hear the quarter-to bell ringing from the old louvred belfry. There was time. Plenty of time. Once his friend, Francis Patrick Hanrahan, used to soar up and down at the end of the bellrope, bouncing between earth and sky, calling the parishioners in an erratic and musical way to mass; now, Popsy knew, it was a tape, loudspeakers, timers; there was no bell, not really. Not any more. A ghost bell, only. Things change.

He stooped his old back and gathered up a handful of sky blue pansies, irises as golden as God's crown, tulips as perfect as the chalice itself. He gathered a fistful of grasses from the edge of his ground. He made a bouquet and tied it all together with the dried-out stem of a daffodil. He was wearing his Sunday suit, a grey suit he had worn every Sunday for over eighteen years, a grey so grey it had begun to darken towards black, the way afternoon eases into dusk. He had no tie. He had never worn a tie. Unnatural thing for a man to have hanging under his chin. He put the bouquet inside his jacket and buttoned it tight. He buttoned and belted his old brown coat. He stooped again and tucked the bottoms of his grey trousers inside his woollen socks, hoisting the socks as high as he could to guard his clothes from the oil and dirt of the bike. For the days turned and turned, would turn until all the spinning stopped and the centre stilled.

Popsy began to whistle. He picked up his bike from where it slept against the wire fence. It was as old as Popsy himself, its black chrome long gone grey, its wheels not quite round, its appurtenances doubtful. But it was faithful, it would serve. Popsy was ready for the world.

His gate hung slightly crooked; he held the bike with his right hand, he pushed the gate with the other. At that moment a sleek black car, a BMW, passed along the road leading away from town. It stopped a few yards beyond Popsy's gate; it was a black panther, its fur agleam, its lithe body idling. The window purred down and Bertholt Dieter Hammerfeld put his head out.

'Ah! You are zare!'

Popsy didn't know if he was zare or not, but he opened his old gate and wheeled his bike onto the road. Popsy was in no hurry. God had eternity. Popsy had time. The Germans were wealthy, retired, they had bought the old Pike Estate. They had money. And time. He closed the gate after him. The demountable squatted where it was. Waiting.

'Gut morning, mister, ahhhh, em . . . *Ja!*'

Popsy was not impressed. 'Good morning. Herr. Grand day, thanks be to God.'

'Grand day. *Ja!* Can vee offer you a lift today?'

Popsy swung his leg over the saddle. 'Ah no, thanks very much but. Wrong direction. Mass is th' other way. And sure I'm used to th' oul' bike.'

He saw the sheen of golden cuff links against the gleaming white sleeves, the ink black suit. The face was a fed face. A finished face. But kind.

'*Gut*, and so. *Slán leat.*' And there was that big sausage laugh while the car moved on, almost soundlessly, the wheels barely dislodging the gravel, a little flourish of exhaust fumes left hanging on the air. *Slán leat*, indeed. More Irish than the Irish themselves. Buying up old porcelain, old donkey carts, tinker caravans, doing them up, selling them again, to other Germans come to gawp and wonder at the things the locals had used up and forgotten. Buying up the world. Popsy's world. And off now for their Sunday whiskeys, followed by Sunday lunch. In Ferndale Lodge. And never a tosser for God . . .

'Hup! Alma!' sang out Popsy. He shoved off. He was in no hurry. He was on God's palm. Breathed-on. Cared-for. Contented.

Cars were parked all over the area in front of the church, red and white cars, green and blue, yellow, pink, black. They were parked on either side of the road, too, making passage difficult. Leaning on hedges, perched on pebble-piles, blocking gateways, as if the citizens of God had universal rights. Popsy sailed gently through the cars on his high, majestic bike. There was silence everywhere. It was a kingly progress.

He leaned the bike against the periphery wall of the church grounds, stooped and drew his trouser legs out of his stockings. Soon, he thought to himself, soon, this young baby priest will have drive-thru masses, like the drive-thru food places they had in the town. Popsy took his bouquet of flowers from inside his jacket and straightened it out, smoothing ruffled petals, untangling stems. There were a few men in the porch, leaning against the wall, grinning as Popsy approached.

Nicky Maguire, small farmer, slouched out into the fresh air. He had a cigarette hanging off his lips and he was fighting with a box of matches.

'Popsy!'

'Good morning, Nicky!'

'How's the lady-friend, Popsy?' (eyeing the flowers).

''Tis for the Virgin, Nicky, the Virgin.'

'No virgins round about these parts, Popsy, if we've got

an'thin' to do with it. Wha'? Hah? Wha'?'

Popsy did not respond. He did not wish to judge.

Nicky got his cigarette going and blew a slow, leisurely cloud into the grey air.

'No ashtrays in the church, Popsy. Wha'?'

'Not yet, Nicky, not yet. Might come soon, though!'

'Ay! some operator, this Father Bellamy. Wha'? Wants us to call him Stephen. Imagine that. Stephen! Me and Stephen. Wha'? Hah? Feels wrong in the mouth, Popsy, feels like chewin' hard green sloes. Wha'?'

Nicky wandered on down the path towards the gate. He might wander back when the cigarette went out.

Father Stephen Bellamy was at his sermon when Popsy began his walk up the centre aisle. Popsy had come to pay his respects to God and Father Stephen Bellamy was not God. Popsy's boots made a sluicing, creaking sound on the new parquet floor. Father Stephen lost the trend of his thought. There was silence in the church while he searched among the seasoned cupboards of his head for the trusted words. Like a juddering car he began again. Popsy lay prostrate before the steps of the altar, in homage to the awesome deity ruling over all. He lay still for a time and God opened His lazy eye to acknowledge his coming. Father Stephen got on with his words.

Here and there among the congregation a young child sniggered. But the elders had seen all this before and they could let it slide right on over them, the way a faint tang in the incense can disturb the senses for a moment before the sweet scent takes over.

Popsy's mind turned on magnificence. He was before the Thunderer, the Iris-maker, the One who ran His hand along a mountainside to create the crags, the One who touched a drop of blood and made the poppy. Popsy's mind did not find words. But it felt right for him to have his face pressed sore against the cold, green marble floor of the world.

Father Stephen harried his words to a premature close and began the Credo. 'IbelieveinGodtheFatheralmighty...' The people shuffled slowly to their feet and the words came out, mumbled, drowsy and unrhythmic. Popsy stood, too, genuflected slowly, then walked around the edge of the sanctuary. He went up to the statue of the Blessed Virgin Mary and placed the flowers at Her feet. He bowed low before Her, overcome again at the thought of Her, a young and beautiful countrywoman become the mother of the great God, the Ganger, the Goldfinch-maker. He sighed aloud with his wonder and longing.

At communion time the people approached the altar and Popsy, standing back into a corner, watched as they stabbed their tongues into the air, long tongues, short tongues, chipped tongues... 'The Body of Christ' 'Amen' repeated over and over as Father Stephen moved rapidly along the lines, like a dunlin dipping and hopping along the edge of the ever-shifting waves, economically stabbing back at the tongues, darting at them as they swallowed down the bones and skin, the head heart feet and blood of the Lord their God. Popsy, knowing sin, would not dare... He knelt on the high marble reaches of the world's strand and bowed his head down, like an ostrich, where he could hide. And his great God nodded, and frowned, and beckoned, and promised...

When Father Stephen left the altar, a murmur of conversation began among the people as they moved slowly out of the church. It was like a wave, withdrawing, leaving high and alone the one great rock that was Popsy Foran. Popsy loved the silence they left behind them, as benches and kneelers, the very floor itself, settled, sighing, back into restfulness. The silence seemed to tremble, to shiver with the luxury of its self-awareness. Popsy remained kneeling on the marble steps, his eyes closed, and God was fumbling still inside his head, knocking and testing, whistling and shuffling, poking His finger into the vulnerable, jelly-fish bones of Popsy's brain.

When God eventually left him alone, Popsy went up to the altar to clear up the little sentences of candlewax that had fallen onto the cloth. He picked them up, cautiously, trying to read them, but he could not. Carefully he stowed them in the pocket of his greatcoat. Father Stephen, dressed in blue jumper, red shirt, grey trousers, sauntered from the sacristy towards him. Father's face was a marble tabernacle; cool; Popsy felt it was time to go.

'There y'are, Father!'

'Yes, Mr Ahhhh . . . Here I am, indeed. Indeed!'

'Just the wax, Father, I do clean it away for you.'

'Thankyou, thankyou.'

'But it's not the same, Father, don't you know, it's not the same at all.'

'What's not the same, Mr Ahhhh . . . ?'

'Nothing, Father.'

'Nothing?'

'There's nothing the same, at all. At all. They've taken the heart out of it, Father.'

'Out of the wax?'

'Out of the mass, Father. Out of the world. They've taken the Latin out of living, if you follow, the ceremony like, they've quenched the high candles and made instant peas out of the hymns; guitars and bongoes and tin whistles where there was the organ, don't ye know? They've brought down the angels out of the sky and put them counting coins on the sacristy counter; they've hidden away the incense and twisted the altar round till we can see only its back. And there's you, Father, if you'll not mind the words, and Herr Whatshisname out of Germany, and there's the big men of the town with their new shops and they're bringing in a whole new world, filled with buttons and handles and computers and exhaust fumes, and their God is in a hurry, I think, before the end of the world might catch Him up. 'Tis a different mountain now they do be wanting to shift. And I find myself on the threshold, Father, and I don't know whether it's coming in I am or going out. And that's the fair truth of it now, Father, the fair truth.'

Shaking his head slowly and sadly, Popsy turned and walked down towards the door. Father Stephen stood where he had been, his hands half lifted, his words unspoken, his resolve dissipating like candle smoke in the stale air of the church.

Outside, a light mist moved thoughtfully over the fields. Popsy shuddered and looked up into the darkened sky. He sighed heavily, stooped to tuck his trouser legs inside his stockings. He got on his bike and headed for home. Meals-on-wheels would be soon. Mash. Mate. Gravy.

The world was wet, sodden and dripping now, but he went slowly. As he topped Doherty's Hill, Popsy's mind was on ordinary things, bread, and bushes, and a warm gas fire. But then, as if the world dimmed and began to shift, Popsy's eyesight gave way, just a little, and the world grew fuzzy about him in a snowstorm of black and white dancing spots. The brakes began to squeak as he went down the hill. There was a strange, sickening click! and the brake-grips were loose in his hands. There was silence as he gathered speed, heading almost blindly into a darkening tunnel, silence except for the gentle, hushing sound of the wheels on the wet road, hush Popsy hush, hush Popsy hush. At the bottom of the hill the road took a sharp dog-leg to the right. A door. A closed door. Popsy lost control and the bicycle slewed suddenly into the middle of the road. Just then a fast, purring BMW came around the corner against him. Soon, only the two bicycle wheels, the front one buckled, were spinning, spinning, spinning in the air, and the rest of the world was silence.

THE COFFIN MASTER

He stopped suddenly, stood still a moment, then glanced carefully up and down the road. At once, like a fox slipping out of view, he had clambered over the stone wall and down the grass bank to the water's lip. Rock River was a mountain stream that here, below the village, had become fat and sluggish. It had golden eels that moved like strings of molten butter; it had tiny mountain trout that never grew larger than his father's thumb but that were vivid and supple and tantalising. The water, dark brown, bubbled thinly over the stones.

Paschal Sweeney slipped in quickly under the bridge. He swung his schoolbag off his back and dropped it onto the concrete base of the bridge. So far, so good. Soon, he thought, summer would begin; soon; he was hovering on the edge, now, of independence.

He stood a while, still as a trout facing upstream. The bridge was a small one, single-arched, low and dark, but high enough for a boy to stand almost wholly upright. The winter was long over and done, the spring rains had been gentle on the world. The stream made a soft, cluck-clucking sound, suggesting warmth and dozing-time and dreamdays. He allowed his eyes to stare at nothing for a while; that way he could let the sounds take him over, he could feel his own existence as a part of the breathing of the island.

Then he blinked, rapidly. He must keep his mind acutely aware of things today. Today of all days. Today he would pass from imagining into act, he would break violently through from childhood into manhood.

He coughed, softly, relishing the way the sound echoed in the dark privacy of the underbridge. He heard a car coming from the direction of the village. He tensed with delighted anticipation. The car passed over the bridge and he sensed the small shivering of the concrete, the way the sound from above had that special quality of closeness and distance at the same time. He trembled with the pleasure of his secrecy, of his crime.

Nobody, ever, played truant from Miss Tighe's class. Nobody. For Miss Tighe had a terrible imagination. She was getting on, Miss Tighe, all the parents said as much, extenuatingly, Miss Tighe is getting on, they said, as if in the hope that in five or ten years' time she would have retired, or be dead, and that ought to be sufficient to compensate the boys for their present sufferings. Miss Tighe, as far as anyone could remember, had always been 'getting on'. She had never been young, Miss Tighe, she couldn't have been. She was of ordinary height. Her hair was always the same, small hand-shakings of hay-coloured wisps, the skull showing through in patches. She was 'getting on'. Her face was grey-coloured, like putty, with little river-maps of red and purple veins high on her cheekbones and a terrifying clump of thin, hay-coloured hair beneath her lower lip. She had a pimple, or a wart, on the right-hand side of her upper lip and it wobbled when she was angry. It wobbled often. She wore glasses, thick-rimmed glasses which magnified her angry eyes. And she wore suits, Miss Tighe, matt-coloured, tight-fitting suits that forced her to walk with short, angry steps.

Under the bridge Paschal shuddered. She always found things out. Miss Tighe. Though Paschal had never missed a day and could be expected to have come down with flu, she would find out. And then ... ! for Miss Tighe's imagination worked uncannily when it came to punishment, the invention of tortures, the adaptation of machinery to the heightening of pain in the bodies of young boys. Punishment, suffering, wonderful things for pushing the reluctant body through fence and thorn-hedge into the wide meadows of truth. Miss Tighe had a cupboard; it stood, innocent, silent, menacing, in the top left corner of the classroom. Stood, like a hangman, in full view of the boys, waiting.

And there were rumours, small histories, whispers. It was as if Miss Tighe had taken love, along with all her childhood toys, and locked them away in an inaccessible attic. Her cupboard was full of genuine, old-fashioned, bamboo canes; she had sticks cut from ash-trees; she even had the new, stitched-leather pandybat. But these were the everyday cups and saucers of schoolroom punishment. For special misdemeanours she invented special punishments. She could stand behind a boy and pull both his ears, hard, until they grew red as flames. She could hoist a boy out of his desk by taking a fistful of his hair. She could bend a boy over and break an ash-stick across the seat of his pants. She could back a boy into a corner, slapping his cheeks all the time, hard, left cheek, slap! right cheek, slap! or concentrate on one cheek until a boy's brains were steaming and whistling with foolishness.

Once she had taken a boy out into the yard and hung him by his wrists to the branch of a tree. He had dangled there for half an hour and spent the rest of the week at home, recovering, suffering the wrath of his father. For fathers and mothers believed, in that dark, sad time, when life was a cross and death was a release, when every day was a Lenten Day and the God of the Fathers was a vengeful, watchful God, that the teacher had a vocation handed down by the Christ, the Pain-Master, and that any boy who was punished by Miss Tighe deserved what he got, and more. And the boys knew that all living is coloured black with sin and the only way to purity and truth was through pain and wonderfully imagined agony. Water the roots of the punishment tree and the soul will flourish with wondrous fruits.

Paschal took his lunch out of his schoolbag. Today he had his usual sandwich, white bread, home-made butter, a slice of cold beef. A bottle of milk stoppered with a twisted spill of newspaper. He had eaten well at breakfast, now he took the slice of beef from the sandwich, broke up the bread and scattered it out onto the stones. For the birds. The tiny birds of paradise, the grey wagtails. And maybe a small brown mountain trout would pucker its little mouth to the surface of the water and swallow down a crumb. He picked off the little threads of fat from the beef and threw them, too, for whatever tiny animal would find and have them.

He chewed the beef, thoughtfully. It was Friday. It was a mortal sin to eat meat deliberately and knowingly on a Friday. His parents had not noticed. He had taken the meat with full deliberation. He could not abide the thought of another sandwich moistened with jam. Today he would need all the strength that meat could give. Anyway, his soul was already signed for delivery into the corridors of hell. What did another sin matter? The beef tasted good, better than ever. He knew a sudden surge of confidence and aggression. Now, his soul damned for ever, hadn't he become a man more certainly than most of those who lounged outside the chapel on Sundays, smoking, gossiping, flinging remarks like mud against the girls? He would face Miss Tighe with his fists clenched.

He drank his milk, too. Later he would be thirsty. He rinsed out the bottle with river water, then filled it, careful not to disturb the silt on the river bed. The water was light brown, almost golden, but it was clear and pure. It would serve.

Still relishing his defiance, Paschal took out his arithmetic copy from his schoolbag, opened it wide and set it to float on the shallow water of the river. For a moment, surprised, it lay on the surface, then, very very slowly, began to move. Paschal prodded at it with his finger and it sank a little, the leaves beginning to curl, to separate. He watched as little curlicues of blue ink lifted from the page and vanished in the water. Numbers, plus signs, multiplication signs. He laughed. If Miss Tighe wanted to see his homework she would have to go to the mouth of Rock River and put all the water through a sieve.

There was a sudden tumbling of stones on the upstream side of the bridge. Paschal leaped upright, terrified, banging the back of his head against the roof of the bridge. He went cold with fright. He saw small stones slip down from the bank into the river. Someone was coming down towards the water. Holding the back of his head with one hand he stood transfixed. He knew it was Granny Julia Wrynne, killed dead as a plank just last week. She was coming from beyond to punish him. She would come in under the bridge, her white hair heavy with dirt, she would reach her long arms out at him, long, bony fingers covered with clay; she would open her awful mouth and breathe the stench of the grave over him. His stomach knotted up, the back of his neck seemed to contract, he tried to scream.

A sheep stumbled down into the water and looked in at him. Its wool was long and heavy with clotted dirt and sheep-shit. Its black face was foolish, its horns short and curled, its eyes big and black and stupid.

'You awful bastard!' Paschal shouted at it. Then he stooped

quickly, gathered up a stone out of the water and flung it at the animal. The sheep ignored stone and boy, crossed the river with complete indifference and disappeared from Paschal's view.

'God forgive me!' he whispered. 'I'm sorry, Granny Julia, I'm sorry. Pray for me, Granny Julia, pray for me.'

He made sure his bag was safely out of the way of the water. He tucked the bottle into one of the pockets of his trousers. Then he stepped back out from under the bridge into the soft sunshine of the morning.

Julia Wrynne had lived always among the dead. They came to her as soon as dusk crept in over the island. She stood, tall and strong as a mountain ash, outside her door, looking down over the island and it was she who was the ghost, standing in her long, white shroud. She had a sprig of palm leaf in her right hand, blessed from Palm Sunday. With it she scattered, north, east, south, west, holy water about the jamb of her door, praying that the evil spirits might stay clear. Then she closed the door and went back into the kitchen of her two-roomed house. There were no bolts or latches on her door, it was an island, after all, terrors happened elsewhere, and no lock or bolt could keep the dead out of a house.

Julia's cottage was perched high along the hillside. During the famine years of the last century the village had quickly fallen away from about the small Wrynne holding. The Wrynnes held on, surviving on winkles, seaweeds, nettle tea, growing skinny and bone-sharp as unfeathered birds, losing their hair and teeth and reason – but surviving. Around them the old abandoned houses disintegrated and the potato ridges slept under decades of hungry grass. Now the long, clay-and-stone road led only to the Wrynne house where Julia lived, alone, among the dead.

She drew her chair close to the fire and sat rocking in the gathering gloom. She knew all the sounds, the shifting of sheep or wind, the falling of rocks high along the mountainside, the knocking of the dead as they searched for their old homes in the long-since disappeared village. She held her rosary in her hands and prayed, the words monotonous as the gentle shifting of the stream on the hillside that wound down past her house to become Rock River before it widened into a shallow, muddy estuary. She knew the cries of the birds that searched the hillside, like herself, for a living: the gulls; the skald crows; the choughs.

And always Julia Wrynne, fifty years old and a thousand years foolish, rocked and mumbled, like the sea working fretfully at the granite cliff-face beyond.

The fire settled quickly into ash. Darkness filled the small room. She sat in her burying shroud and listened for the footsteps of the kindly dead. At last she sighed, feeling the fingernails of the cold mountain night touch on her paper-thin flesh. The dead she loved, and she loved, too, the children that came rollicking and mocking and offering their help to her house high along the hillside. She knew, for she was foolish but no fool, that she was an adventure in their small, curtailed lives.

'Granny Julia, Granny Julia, any jobs for us? Any jobs?'

She would hustle out to them, suggest a bit of weeding in her kitchen-garden, she would set them picking gooseberries, or rhubarb, or cabbage, planting and harvesting her potatoes, or running the two miles down, the two miles back, from MacHenry's General Store, for messages, and sixpence for yourself, there's a wonderful young boy! And when they were finished, jostling and grinning and nudging one another forward, she brought them boxty bread, hot and flavoursome and rich, the yellow butter drooling over them and lovely green flakes of fresh parsley scattered on their flesh.

'There now, childers, ate them up! I'll put hairs on yer chests an' backs an' chins an' 'll make fine min outa ye, 'll turn the heads of all the lovely girleens searchin' for gossoons to bring into their beds. Grand childers, good boys, good boys...'

Her own, poor, hard-baked womb had never known the hungers of any child, whatever her dreams or fantasies may have been. But who ever knows? who knows? when she lay alone at night stretched out on her solitary, unwarm bed, longing and waiting and dozing, prepared, in her burying shroud, who knows how many of the dead had come in to her, offering their subtle bodies, their perfumes of decay, their seeds of everlasting peace?

'Granny Julia, Granny Julia, Granny Julia...'

Paschal Sweeney often visited the house on the side of the hill. When she came out in her big boots, her black woollen stockings, her heavy skirts, her dark cardigans, her aprons, her face would be a small light of happy foolishness.

'An' who do ye be today, gossoons? who do ye be today?'

'Tom Mix, Granny Julia.'

'Hopalong Cassidy.'

'Buffalo Bill.'

'Buck Jones.'

And she would laugh her flowery potato laugh and rub her hands together in delight.

'An' Paschal Sweeney, is he not with ye the day?'

'No, Granny Julia, we're Tim Nulty's gang.'

Tim Nulty's gang got the harder jobs, the digging, heaving, clearing, the hauling of buckets of water down from the corrie up above, the fetching of flower and bacon and porridge oats up from MacHenry's General Store. And pennies handed out, and halfpennies, and half-stale home-made bread.

'An' ye? who do ye be today, gossoons? who do ye be today?'

'Ivan Ivanovich, Granny Julia!'

'Ostap Feodorovitch.'

'Andrii Vasilievsky Ostroff.'

'Basavriuk.'

'We're the Tatars and the Cossacks, Granny Julia!'

'Ah ha!' she screeched, 'my favourites! my own very favourite gossoons!'

And she would set them the easy tasks, the washing of a head of cabbage, the chasing of sheep from the lower field, the clearing of a few more small stones from the small meadow. For she would sit and yarn with them, feeding them well with boxty bread and buttermilk and maybe a biscuit or two from the old brown tin, she would sit down with them on the rocks that formed her boundary wall and listen to their tales.

'I do enjoy them yarns of quare, far places, an' them awful, heavy names. Tell me, Paschal . . .'

'Not Paschal, Granny Julia, my name is Taras Bulba!'

'Taras Bulba? there's a name for ya now!'

'I'm a Cossack, you see. From Russia.'

'Russia! there's a place. Communists an' rednecks an' all!'

'Not rednecks, Granny Julia, you're thinking of redskins. Redskins are Indians. There's no Indians in Russia. Cowboys and Indians, that's Tim Nulty's gang. We're Tatars and Cossacks. Patcho Whelehan told us . . .'

'Patrick Joseph Whelehan, is it? the coffin master himself? Poor fella, poor fella.'

'You see, Granny Julia, the Cossacks are warriors. On horses. And we accept no insults! When we meet we have a fight.'

'A fight? That sounds awful rough.'

'It's not, really. It's our way of saying hello. We live in the Ukraine. We're letting our hair grow long and we fight the Turks, and the Mussulmans.'

'The muscle *men*, Paschal, the muscle men. Not mans. Men.'

'No, no, Granny Julia, the Mussulmans. I think. That's what Patcho calls them. And I'm Taras Bulba. Wherever there's a hillock there's a Cossack. Ostap here, he's a Sotnik, he's commander of a hundred Cossacks. And we have a lot of hetmans. They're the chiefs.'

'Head*men*, Paschal, headmen. Not headmans.'

'ok, Granny Julia. Anyway, we never turn down a dare. Patcho tells us we must take up the challenges of life and never turn down a dare. We hunt the Tatars. They're all over the mountain here. All over. And they've horses fast as the wind. And we wear belts and we're all going to grow great big moustaches.'

'That'll be nice, Paschal, I love a man with a nice moustache.'

'I'm Taras Bulba, Granny Julia, and in the story Patcho told us I get captured in the end. And tortured. But I tell them nothing. And then I get crucified.'

'Crucified? Oh my good God!'

'Crucified, yes, upside down, and when I won't die for them they set fire to me. And then I die. I think.'

'That's not very nice, Paschal, that sounds very sore. I wonder at Pat Joe Whelehan to be tellin' ye yarns the likes a' them. Isn't Pat Joe a caution, now I ask ye? a caution to the world out!'

She watched them, hunting round her old house and fields, in and out through the stones of the abandoned village, shooting, screaming, skulking, Paschal giving the orders, whooping on their horses across the steppes of the island hillside.

'Come on,' she had said one day, 'come on, young Paschal Sweeney. I want to show ye what Pat Joe Whelehan done for me.'

She led him slowly around the side of the house, across the

rough-stone yard at the back, towards a small shed that stood at the far corner of her yard. Above them, the sides of the mountain sloped gradually, the lazy-beds, the heather ridges, the erratics. It was a sunny, still afternoon, yet up here there was a breeze. A kestrel hovered on his mattress of air high above. Sheep lay and stirred and over the furthest ridge of the hill the Atlantic Ocean gleamed. There were pipits making their little chirping calls in the distance and the sound of the ocean could be heard as a soft and gentle monotone beyond.

The old woman stopped at the door of the shed. She searched through the deep folds of her skirts. The cowboys of Tim Nulty's gang, the Cossacks of Paschal Sweeney's, had always thought this shed just another abandoned heap of stones, filled with absence and stale air. But Julia produced a key and Paschal saw a bolt high on the old wooden door. There was a new lock on the door. Julia turned, the key held in her hand like a trophy.

'You're a good boy, Paschal Sweeney,' she said, her old face animated, her old brown eyes alight. 'And you're a good friend of Pat Joe Whelehan. And you'll promise me now never, ever, ever to tell a living body about what I've got in here.'

'I promise, Granny Julia, I promise. And Patcho says no Cossack could ever break an oath and if you did you were tied to the pillar of shame and everybody that passed you by had to give you a thump with a heavy club until you were dead. That's what Patcho said. To make it even. To level things . . .'

'Well, now, them Cossacks are real buckos . . .'

The old woman turned the key in the lock and slid back the bolt on the door of the shed. She heaved at the old timbers and the door opened inwards, with loud groans. Paschal could see only a gathering of darkness within. But the old woman was excited, urging him inside before her, pushing him. He rubbed his eyes, blinking hard. She pushed the door as fully open as possible. There was a smell of earth and dampness, an old, old smell.

The old woman stepped into the shed, out of the light. And slowly, as his eyes grew used to the blackness, Paschal could make out what it was she wanted him to see. Raised on two low, wooden struts, about knee-high, was a coffin, taking up almost the whole length of the shed. He could see the beautifully polished wood, gleaming now in the reluctant light. He could see the perfect sheen on the brass handles fixed along the side. He saw the absolute perfection of the coffin shape, the smooth joints in the wood, the complete balance of the long, boat-like form. He could make out the coffin lid standing separately, upright, against the stones of the back wall. He could see the great, brass crucifix, the screws shaped like small crosses. He could see the nameplate already in place. He could read:

JULIA BERNADETTE WRYNNE
Rest in Peace

'It's a coffin!'

The old woman grinned at him. 'Pat Joe made it for me. Specially.'

'But . . . you're not dead?'

'Not yet, not yet, but one day I'll be dead and Pat Joe will make sure I'm put in there and carried down the mountain in it. Look' – and she was moving her hand gently along the inside of the coffin – 'he's made it all soft and comfy inside, the cushions, the satin, the silk . . . All posh and rich, like a queen's!'

'But you have no date written on it . . .'

'Who cares about dates? When you're dead you're dead and you're nothing more to do with dates. And the coffin'll rot more slowly nor me and the crucifix will slide down slow onto my breast and it'll sink into me and I'll be in Paradise then for ever!'

She was moving her fingers lovingly around the edge of the coffin.

'I'm showing you this, Paschal Sweeney,' she said quietly, 'so that you'll know it's where I'm to be laid when I'm took. Just in case something happens poor Pat Joe before me. Do you understand, this is our secret now, yours, and mine, and Pat Joe Whelehan's? I'm putting a great promise on you now, an oath, you're not to tell a body, not till I'm gone. Promise me, Paschal Sweeney, promise me now, there's a boy!'

'I promise.'

'Good boy, good boy,' she said. She was reaching again into the folds of her skirts. 'Take these few shillings now for yourself.'

She produced a carefully folded, yellow-golden ten shilling note, a great treasure before the young boy's eyes.

'I lie in there, son,' she said, looking into the white silk innards of the box. 'I lie in there, the door closed, the darkness about me, I listen to the mountain winds and I feel the emptiness of the whole world, the wide emptiness, and I know for sure we'll all be part of that big emptiness, you and me and Pat Joe, and that's the emptiness Jesus Christ on His cross will fill for me years and years after they have laid me in the soft heart of the earth.'

She caught Paschal's hand and pressed the ten shilling note into his palm.

'You'll be like a son to me, Paschal Sweeney,' she said, vehemently, happily, 'and Pat Joe Whelehan will be like a husband to me and you'll be all I'll ever need in this world, husband, and son, and one of ye, or both of ye, will see me safely laid between the great and kindly hands of God.

★

Julia Wrynne slept among the dead. The world had left her fields, her yard, her house, and a moon had lifted itself over the ridge and stood shadowing the mountainsides. Now and then a snipe lifted and shot itself through the wall of gloom. Sometimes a curlew, away in a damp valley, cried out its joyful cry that, carrying across the wet and lonely places, was translated into a call of sorrow. Julia lit no lights. She took off her skirts and woollens, washed her face and hands in the cold water of the sink. She let her old, grey hair fall loose from its knots and pins. She put on her long, buttermilk-coloured shroud, her bridal dress with the face and heart of Christ Jesus Crucified embroidered on the breast. She sat down by the hearth to wait for the tiredness to come. She held herself about the knees and leaned forward into her dreams. The old house was full of ghosts.

'I know you're there,' she said to them, quietly, moving her body gently on the chair. 'I know you're there, Nora Coyne. Peg-Anne Lynch. John James Dineen. Seamus Pat Michael. Máire Bhán. Seán Lynchehaun . . .'

The buttery light of the moon touched the glass of her small window and sent a soft cobweb of light onto the stone floor. There was a faint sound in the distance, an engine, unreal and out of place along the reaches of the mountainside. Julia heard and paused. Then continued her conversation.

'You are there, I remember you, I miss you. And I know I will be satisfied. Oh Christ, my Christ, 'tis You have placed the longing in my heart and You will not make a fool out of me.'

A cloud slipped across the face of the moon and the sheen of light on her floor disappeared. A black van had stopped down at the foot of the mountain, where the stone and clay track turned from the island road and began up the slope towards the abandoned village. Two men sat in the cabin of the van.

'This is a right fuckin' dump of a place, Kane,' one of them said, the sound of his voice echoing tinnily in the dark den of the van. He was a small man, round-faced, balding, the black stubble of an uncared-for beard shadowing his face. The second man, at the wheel, was younger, with a shock of fawn-coloured hair rising on his head in curls. He seemed to be grinning, his shaven face clean and almost handsome.

'Everything about this island stinks,' Kane answered. 'We'll do our job and get the hell out of it quick as we can.'

'Think we should turn up here, Kane?'

The stone track looked uninviting, leading upwards through the blackness of the mountainside.

'There's one oul' cunt livin' up there, all be herself, Madden,' Kane muttered. 'Not a house in miles, I'm told. Th' oul' cunt must have cash and maybe silver an' stuff an' what good is it to her, wha'? One oul' cunt. It's too easy, Madden, easy as squeezin' shit out of a dead goose.' He laughed, startling his older companion.

Kane turned the wheel of the van with determination and began to urge the whining machine up the slope. Madden reached for the dashboard, holding on as the van lurched and shook on the stones and through the ruts of the track.

'Fuckin' place should be dynamited into hell,' he said, gazing out at the shadowed hillocks and black pools of the hillside.

'We'll leave our mark on it anyhows,' Kane said, laughing raucously, his face peering through the windscreen, following the meagre clarity offered by the headlamps. The van juddered and rebelled, the gears retched and whined, the chassis scraped against boulders.

'Fuck!' Kane spat, 'an' fuck again. And then fuck!'

'This oul' cunt'd better be worth the effort.' Madden's face was red with anger. 'How in the name of Christ could any human being live up here?'

Julia heard the unfamiliar sound rising along the mountain.

'Ssssshhh!' she whispered to her ghosts. A big smile made her eyes brilliant in the darkness.

She watched as a small pane of light, sickly-yellow, appeared high on the wall of her room and moved slowly, crossing over the old dresser with its mugs and plates, coming down the wall gradually, disappearing again. She heard the sounds of the van close to the house. Then there was silence, a long, deep silence, with only the mountain breeze rising from the ice-cold waters of the corrie, brushing against the crags, shivering the roots of heathers and probing the stones of Julia Wrynne's old home. She shivered a moment, then began to rock herself gently as she felt the dead approaching the door of her house.

Kane and Madden sat a while in the van, lights switched off, engine killed. Madden smoked anxiously. Kane watched the house, his eyes half-shut. 'Must be in bed already,' he murmured, 'no light about.'

The mountain breeze touched the van, probing it for its weak points where it could invade and work but the dark, squat shape was alien to this place. Madden shivered. 'Fuckin' cold as the grave up here,' he complained.

Carefully Kane opened the door of the van and stepped out. The ground was soft and he could feel his shoes sink a little in the mud. Anger gripped him. Madden came round the van and stood beside him for a moment. They were black shapes skulking against the blackness of the night, blacker than the darkness about them. Madden gazed out over the mountainside. Far below he could make out a faint light here and there from houses scattered in the valley.

'Let's get this fuckin' business over with,' he hissed, flicking the butt of his cigarette into the night.

They shoved at the door and it opened to them. For a moment they saw nothing inside the darkness of the house. Then they heard a strange, shuffling sound from the room and saw her, risen from the darkness and standing, swaying, a tall, ghostly shape, arms reaching out towards them.

'Jesus!' Madden hissed, grabbing the shoulder of the younger man with his claw-like fingers.

'Jesus! Jesus! Jesus!' whispered the ghostly shape, the words coming soft as a prayer across the darkness. 'Come,' said the old woman, 'you're welcome. Welcome. I'm ready. I'm coming, coming, coming,' and she moved slowly towards them, her arms reaching, her body swaying in its shroud, her face invisible in the darkness.

'Jesus!' Madden hissed again. Kane's hand moved swiftly to his pocket. Even in the darkness of the house the blade flashed and gleamed. Kane leaped suddenly and drove the blade deep into the flesh of the advancing figure. She gasped, and bent forward, and he struck again, and again, and again. She stumbled and fell at last, her hands reaching, her gasps and moans soft and failing. Then she stretched out fully at Kane's feet, twitched a little, and went still. There was silence.

'Fuckin' oul' bat!' Kane muttered.

'You killed her?' Madden said, a soft question, without reproach.

'A batty oul' bitch, that's all!' Kane said.

Their voices sounded loud in the house, loud and unreal and distant. Madden stood at the door, the mountain wind still reaching for him. Kane took out a torch and they moved quickly through the house, stepping over the body on the floor. Rapidly they searched the two rooms, the torch leaping and shifting behind the two small windows of the house and through the open door, flashing like a tiny fire on the hillside, like a shifting will-o'-the-wisp across the boglands. They found nothing. They tore through her clothes, they broke the delft, they rifled through her potato-piles, her bed, her chair.

There was nothing.

'Fuckin' oul' bat!' Kane cursed, 'fuckin' oul' bat!'

After a few minutes Madden stopped.

'There's a shed outside,' he said. 'We'll take a look in there and then get the hell out a' here.'

They went out, leaving the door ajar. The breeze moved in, gently touching the shroud that glistened softly in the darkness. Kane and Madden crossed the yard, the torch throwing a pale yellow light ahead of them.

'Fuckin' door's locked!' Kane said, surprised.

Madden found a rock and flung it hard.

'Must be somethin' special th' oul' bat kept in there!' Kane said, delight and anticipation making him tremble.

Again and again Madden hefted and flung the rock. The door shattered, the rusty hinges yielding, the wood falling away like paper. Kane directed the torch inside and they stepped through the shattered door. The coffin stood, shining and polished before them, the brasses brilliantly reflecting their torchlight.

'Oh holy fuckin' hell!' Kane shouted. Then he turned and ran, back across the yard, dropping the torch on the ground where it lay, still lit, its weak beam calling out from the darkness of the shed. Madden stared a moment, stiff with terror, at the open coffin, as if he expected something to rise up out of it and clutch his throat. Then he turned and ran back across the yard.

On the lower reaches of the hillside a man stood, watching the faint shiftings of a light on the mountainside. He heard the slamming of doors, the quick, urgent spluttering of an engine. He watched as the headlamps bumped and veered along the mountain track. They reached the road and turned north, towards the high, far reaches of the island. He listened intently as the sound of the engine faded away into the silence of the night.

Paschal Sweeney shivered again, remembering his sudden fright as the sheep had clattered out of daylight into his vision. He'd have to be stronger than that, he knew, much stronger, to be able to face the business of this day.

Cautiously he climbed out of the ditch, up the bank, onto the road. There were no sounds of traffic. He looked up and down the road – not a body to be seen. Somewhere, far down in the village, a cock crowed. Up the road to his left, about a quarter of a mile away, he could see the great absence, the black gap that had been MacHenry's General Store. He knew, if he were to walk up there, that little whirlpools of black ash would still rise about his feet and underneath that ash would be skulking the little orange and scarlet creatures that were the devil's emissaries, their mouths agape with flames, their eyes red-black holes, their faces leering with wickedness. It seemed years ago, that wonderful, terrible fire. Years. But it was only three nights ago. Three nights . . . and so much had happened.

He ducked back down to the edge of the river. He glanced once more under the bridge to make sure his bag was safe. Then he began to make his way upriver, towards the low hills, towards Granny Julia's house. Dead Granny Julia. Buried Granny Julia. Murdered Granny Julia. He stopped again, shaken once more by the shock of that awful word, *murder*. How all this world seemed quickly rotten through and through with evil. And what might they not do to him, now, should they catch him in what he was about?

When the news of Julia's murder touched the school, even Miss Tighe's glowering presence could not stop the small breeze of their whispers growing into a storm. A heavy weight of ice seemed to take hold of Paschal's body. All that day he trembled, unable to concentrate on lessons, on Miss Tighe's scoldings and complaints. During breaktime the boys all stood together, shaken and stunned, in a corner of the yard, all united for a while in their fear and loss. There were rumours, many rumours; it was a flock of starlings startled suddenly out of a wood at dusk, each starling an explanation, each black feather a definite fact.

As soon as he could, after school, Paschal had run all the way to Julia Wrynne's cottage. He wondered if the people knew about the coffin, he could tell them, he would have to tell them. He had promised. When he got there he could see there were people, lots of people, some mumbling together in little groups outside. He heard the word 'murder' repeated over and over. So, it was true! He went to the door of the cottage and peered into its dark heart. He could hear a low hum of prayers, the women were there, mumbling the ritual words, each one of them seized by the sudden and awful fact. Gradually his eyes got used to the gloom. The coffin was there, up on the kitchen table, the women gathered about it, men in the corners, all of them at prayer. Paschal moved cautiously to the table. The coffin looked so right there, on her table, and she looked so right, lying inside it, the ghost of a smile on her putty-like face, the gentle old hands folded over the crucifix on her breast, the edges of the shroud just visible under the silken border the coffin master had so carefully prepared. Except – she was so still, so terribly, terribly still. Paschal watched her face a while, convinced the eyes must move, the lips must tremble, the nostrils twitch. But there was nothing, absolutely nothing.

An old woman near him intoned suddenly: 'Eternal rest grant unto her O Lord . . .'

And suddenly Paschal cried out loud, he shrieked, with the terrible wrongness of it, the darkness, the loneliness, the gentleness that had been suddenly taken away, the warm bright core of their lives become so quickly a used-up and abandoned quarry. He put his two fists up to the sides of his head and he shrieked, a helpless, animal plea.

The people were startled.

'Holy Mother of Divine Grace!' one of the women said. A man got up quickly and held him by the shoulders, essaying comfort. And then the women started to keen, released by the cry. At first it was a low wail, a distant suggestion of thunder. Paschal stood, enthralled and appalled as the sound gathered about him. He could scarcely make out the words, spoken and chanted in Irish. Woe, woe, woe, sorrow and loss and woe! Words filled with a restrained energy, the energy of despair, words that flowered in the gloom around him with a huge, scarlet blossoming. The people released their anguish, their mirror-image lying on the table before them, they were letting their fear of death, their fear of all strange and dangerous forms that enter life suddenly and tear it apart, loose into the black air about the coffin.

'Dead! And gone for ever! Oh woe, sorrow, woe ...'

The words began to rise in pitch and volume and suddenly the young boy felt overwhelmed by the age of the people surrounding him, by their stale smells, their dark faces, as if the colour of the clay were beginning to break out from under their flesh; he could see the knuckles of their twisted fingers gripping to life on the top of their crude walking sticks, he could see the gapped and broken and empty mouths as they opened and closed, the spittle hanging about their lips. The words merged in his ears into a rising howl and he knew suddenly, he knew that they were keening for him, keening for Paschal Sweeney, because it was he who was dead, who would be buried for ever, here, in this gloom, among all these people already dead.

He backed away, bewildered and in terror, pulling himself

away from the hands that held him. He reached the door. His fingers touched the paper-dry flesh of an old woman's face and he imagined she turned a fanged mouth towards him; he gasped and moved backwards and felt something firm behind him and when he turned to grasp it, it was the coffin lid, standing like a quiet, amused stranger against the wall, sardonic, certain, suave. The noise gathered about him, rose rapidly towards a sky filled with a fever of despair and loss and he screamed out the name of the only person he thought could save him: 'Patcho! Patcho! Patcho!'

Strangely then, the voices wavered, they dribbled down into near-silence, only a few murmured phrases passed like spirits through the gloom.

Two strong hands were on Paschal's shoulders, holding him, turning him, and he looked up into the grey, angry face, into the red, watery eyes of old Micheál Woods.

''Twas Patcho done it, Paschal,' the old voice hissed down at him, the breath smelling of foulness and tobacco juice, ' 'twas Patcho Whelehan, 'twas the coffin master murdered the poor old woman!'

The strong hands pushed and guided him towards the small rectangle of light that was the doorway and he was shoved out into the fresh mountain air of late afternoon.

Paschal climbed steadily now along the banks of Rock River. The morning remained fine. It was good to be out in the world, his feet touching the moss-soft ground, his hands clutching the tough stems of heather for support. How different from the stale indoor horror of the schoolroom. He jumped lightly from one bank of the stream to the other. How they all hated Patcho Whelehan! he knew that. They hated him, their coffin master, because he had never become their slave, he had never fallen down to grovel before them, to apologise, to serve them. Because he had moved away from them as from some rottenness, refusing to acknowledge their power over him, their authority over one who was broken but who would not yield.

'I am their nightmare,' Patcho told him once, 'I am their nightmare and they are frightened of the light I cast about me in the day.'

Paschal turned. He was standing on a high bank of the river. He was already well up along the lower reaches of the mountain and the island was beginning to lay itself out at his feet like a lazy, marmalade cat. Sun-blessed. The shadows of clouds moving lazily over. He could see for miles in every direction. And always the ocean, beautiful, visible now in every direction from where he stood, wrapping the island in its embrace.

The black ruins of MacHenry's General Store were ugly and intrusive below him.

'It's like a beautiful woman's smiling mouth,' Paschal said to himself, endeavouring to follow Patcho's exhortations. 'Smiling – but with one black gap showing.'

Use your imagination, Patcho had told him, it lifts you out of the stone fields of the island into meadows of endless possibilities.

That Patcho'll turn your head, the others said to him, the adults, the field-plodders, the low-road travellers, he'll turn your head like a screw till it falls off your neck onto the ground.

He had been fast asleep that night when the clamour woke him. A dark night, with a few stars sharp as thorns across the sky. He lay in the darkness of his room, wondering what it was that had lifted him awake. Then he heard the shouting, voices calling to one another, urgently. He went to the window and drew back the curtain. And saw it at once, the store in flames, the orange and scarlet flames, the great bursts of vermilion sparks. In the sickly light the conflagration shed he could see figures moving frantically about, demon-spirits on the shores of hell.

Quickly he put his pants and jumper on over his pyjamas, tied his boots over his naked feet and ran downstairs. The front door of his house was wide open. He began to run towards the wondrous spectacle. Then, as he ran between the high dark shapes of old trees, he stopped. What if this was but another dream? another nightmare? He had been having so many lately, ever since the murder, strange, tangible dreams that left him exhausted when he woke up, and sometimes nightmares, wild, terrifying nightmares that brought him suddenly awake and left their images hurting his head like a taste of sickness left long after in the mouth. Granny Julia Wrynne cackled her way through those dreams. Old men and women threw clay down on him in his wet, cold grave. Patcho Whelehan raised an axe above his bowed head. Paschal thumped himself now on the forehead. He shook his head. He spoke aloud, to the trees.

'I am awake. It's night-time. There's a fire in the store. I'm awake.'

Convinced, he whooped with excitement and ran on again, faster than before.

His parents were there, with other neighbours, and several children. Paschal moved swiftly among them, identifying, questioning. They stood in a small yard across the road from the store. The three floors were on fire, wildly, hopelessly, brilliantly on fire. The flames were moving through the doors and windows of the ground floor, the shop, the family home. He could see them dance and frolic through the rooms on the second floor, it was like watching a great ballroom dance behind windows. On the top floor, Patcho's floor, he could see the flames working their devastation. He looked about him. Mr MacHenry and his wife, wearing slippers and dressing gowns, stood together, watching. Their faces were white as the faces of the dead. Near them stood Camillus MacHenry, a boy in Paschal's class, rotund, aggressive, bullying. He stood in his pyjamas, unsure whether to be pleased with the wonderful spectacle of their great store gone up in flames, or whether he should cry.

There was an explosion and several windows on the second floor blew out. The fire seemed to leap out through the windows with renewed cheering and blackened the walls outside. The yard about the witnesses was lit up bright as a summer's day. The noise was awesome. Paint tins exploded in the shop. Canisters of gas blew up. One gable wall seemed to bulge impossibly. The adults moved fretfully about, uncertain what to do, how to react. The fire brigade had been sent for but it could be an hour before they arrived. It was hopeless.

Someone screamed.

'Patcho! It's Patcho! Up there! Look, look! It's Patcho!'

Paschal looked up. The flames had burst through the windows of the top floor and were melting the lead on the roof. For a moment he could see the figure of a man waving his arms frantically from one of the top floor windows. The crowd fell deathly silent. The flames whooshed and hissed and burned. Patcho had disappeared since the police had discovered Granny Julia's body all laid out in its coffin on the table of the house. Now here he was, in his own place, and his place was on fire. He was afloat on a sea of flames.

Paschal thought he heard a long, tortured scream. Then Patcho's figure vanished from the window. For a moment longer Paschal stood, petrified with horror. And then it seemed as if a great red flame took him over and he screamed a high-pitched, long-drawn-out scream of loss and terror. He moved forward towards the vast inferno. He was still screaming.

'Don't go near it, Paschal,' his father said, holding him firmly by the shoulder. 'Don't go near it. It's hopeless. The place is as wild as hell.'

Paschal tried to struggle free. 'Patcho's in there!' he yelled, 'you'll have to save him!'

They held him then, more firmly. And he yielded to them, suddenly, and sat down heavily on the ground. The fire was rampaging among all the coffins and timbers of the coffin master's world, the sawdust, the wood-chips, the planings, the glues, the varnishes, the stains. It would melt the brass nameplates with the inscribed RIPs, it would lick up the small brass cross-topped screws, it would swallow whole the brass crucifixes, the round, hinged brass handles. It would devour the coffin master himself, chewing him, digesting him wholly, in its disdain.

For a long time the fire danced and roared, its yelling, un-hampered havoc terrifying to behold. The timbers of the roof caved in and great volcanoes of sparks flew high against the stars. And soon the second floor, too, caved in, the house im-ploding under the violence of its conflagration and once again great geysers of flame rose, renewed, against the night. The watching ghosts were still, awed and silenced before the terrific force that had been let loose amongst them. And then the gable wall fell out, down into the yard below and the great structure of MacHenry's General Store itself seemed to sigh, and yield, and collapse onto itself. And still the fire burned on, insatiable.

Paschal thought he remembered hearing someone whisper 'Patcho, poor, poor Patcho. Poor, lost, soul.'

And was it a dream, or a nightmare, that somebody else re-sponded, in a half-guilty, awed whisper: 'It's justice, that's what it is! The wrath of God strikes quickly down where a ter-rible murder has been done!'

Standing now, high above the island fields in their

innocence, their quiet, purring gentleness, Paschal shuddered again at the memory of that night. Oh the fools! he thought, the fools! how wrong they can be, the adults, how wrong and blind and stupid they can be!

Then he turned again, facing upriver, for he had things to do today that no adult would ever be able to do.

Nobody ought to take a shotgun to his mouth and snuggle in to its perfection. Kissing it. On the mouth. Nobody ought to take a shotgun to his eye and watch down into the bottomless well of its darkness. A shotgun. Or a rifle. Loaded. Alive and menacing. All of that ought to go without saying. That's why it was never said. At least not in Pat Joe Whelehan's hearing.

Patcho was not a tall man. But he had been handsome, trim, swarthy, strong. He strode the island like a king, his chest criss-crossed by cartridge-belts, shotgun belted over his shoulder, .22 under his right arm. He was exuberant, ebullient, a killer, a leveller, a prince. He worked in MacHenry's General Store as handyman, heaver of grain-sacks, master of tools and timbers, his eye perfect to the balancing, his snort of mockery quick before any man hesitant over type of wood or name for drill and bit. And the younger women eyed him, cautiously yet long-ingly, for the balance of life seemed heavily weighted on Pat Joe Whelehan's side.

On the mountain slopes Patcho shot partridge and pheasant, and sometimes, too, a mountain goat. He had a large, hunter's satchel slung over his left shoulder and he came home with it full, always. The leather claws of a pheasant, the cotton wool scut of a rabbit, sometimes the long, quill-like bill of a snipe, all these protruded from the sack in silent homage as he strode home. He stalked, and skulked, and lurked. He dropped slowly onto one knee, as if genuflecting before the majesty of the world, but keeping the rabbit-warren in his sights, or the head-high innocence of a pheasant, and then he aimed, holding the creature erect, watchful and ignorant in the sights for as long as he dared. He exulted in that long moment of waiting; he was – God – for that length of time, with power over life and death, and he breathed deeply, content, assured. When he came striding down the long valley homewards, his satchel bulging, or a goat slung carelessly over his back, the whole island seemed to be at his feet, grovelling in salutation. He whistled then, masterful, cock, in tune. And sometimes, from the grim darkness of her house, Julia Wrynne gazed out at him as he passed. She sighed, and wished, and dreamed impossible dreams.

Julia was a slave, then, and she knew it, still young enough to wear hope like a ribbon in her hair. But her life, dulled and laborious on the almost barren slopes, stretched out before her, void of purpose, mere existence being the sole object of all her labours. When Pat Joe passed, beautiful as a god, and when her dreams lifted her for a moment from the chicken-trodden earth of her yard, she felt that she could yet be satisfied, and more, much more that satisfied, should he ever turn to her in his need. She had bread enough, potato bread, and meat; what she needed was poetry, more than meat or bread, and Pat Joe Whelehan was the great epic poem the mountainside was singing.

But the only lover that Patcho took was his shotgun, and his .22. After the swift, wild embrace of the gun, after the release, the kill, he would run his hand up along the barrel, along the smooth, still hot, metal, he would handle the finely carved, polished wood of the stock, and sometimes, after an exceptional kill – a mountain goat, a wild duck on the wing, a leaping hare – he would put the warm lips of the gun to his own moist lips, and close his eyes, and kiss. At that moment he knew with absolute certainty that he could rely wholly on himself and on his guns, to see life through, to rule the world and subdue it, to have it lie, panting and humiliated, at his feet.

So the island people came to fear, and ultimately to despise, Pat Joe Whelehan. Secretly they longed for the stealthy, slow movement of God's equalising justice to be manifested in his flesh before them.

One day, then, Patcho set out in the early afternoon, shotgun in his hands, rifle braced about his back, music in his head and a great surge of longing to make his fingers tingle. Down in Harte's meadows there was a pheasant, Patcho knew, a cock pheasant, a dandy, pipe-playing, secretive boyo Patcho was determined to overcome. The afternoon sun was one of God's fairest; the sea blue and still, the slopes waltzing under the shadows of drifting clouds, the skylarks layering the air with music. The world was a gift, offered on the palm of God. The calm and equilibrium of harmony. The world obedient, as it always is, to God's willing.

Patcho stood perfectly still under the shadow of a mountain ash. He stood so quietly he could have been part of that perfect landscape. Waiting, the way a cat will wait, still as the grass about it, the eyes wide open, the body quivering. Until he heard that sudden raucous *huzzah!* from the pheasant, followed by the quick flurry of heavy wings. He raised the shotgun and aimed towards the golden, furze hedgerow. Almost at once the great bird appeared, the glamour of his plumage striking against the green of the meadow grass. His eye bright. His head alert. His chest taut under an array of multipatterned medals. His tail a miracle of self-aggrandisement and glory. Patcho held him in his sights for a long, satisfying moment, then he fired.

The bird was lifted from the grass and flung back against the thorns. It flapped its wings a little, its body twitched, the claws grasping frantically at emptiness. Shocked. Astonished at the undignified, unheralded approach of death. It uttered a faint moan of surprise and pain. Then lay still. Patcho grinned.

'Up ya boyyah!' he muttered aloud. He lifted the shotgun barrel to his lips and kissed the hot, smoking mouth. The excitement kept his body in a tremble. He had forgotten the second cartridge. The shotgun returned his kiss, taking half his lips and the jaw and cheekbone on the right side of his face in the passion of its embrace, flinging the three fingers of his left hand into the air. Patcho was thrown backwards, catching his right leg against the trunk of the ash tree. He crumpled up on the ground, on his side of the field, opposite the burst-open body of the pheasant.

It was Julia Wrynne who found him. She had been watching from the high landscape of her own life. She had heard the shotgun blast. And then she had seen Patcho step from under the tree. She had heard the second blast and had seen Patcho flung down out of his standing onto the green earth. Whimpering and chattering she had hoisted the broken body onto her shoulders and had staggered and stumbled back to MacHenry's General Store, the hot blood of Pat Joe Whelehan dripping over her the way his own birds would drip their life's blood onto the grass from the lip of his hunting satchel.

One Saturday afternoon Patcho sat, a rock among rocks, at the ocean's edge. Behind him low cliffs cut him off from the world of fields, roads, small homes, men. He had learned that he who takes up the sword shall perish by the sword. And he who survives the sword shall perish slowly, with drawn-out pain, on the cross of his own making. Patcho was not acceptable now among ordinary folk. That caved-in, scarred, ugly face. The left hand a mess of flesh and fingers and stumps. The saliva bubbling along the torn lips. The eye, blood-shot and small, that had looked too far in beyond the secret of suffering.

Over the island hung a delicate stillness, a bright silver-and-blue haze of warmth and laziness, a peace out of which the distant village sound of a crowing cock came only as a promise of further quietness. Below him the sea heaved gently against the rocks, like an animal glad to be rubbing its bulk, for comfort, against something more solid than itself. The sun warm on his smitten body, embracing him still.

Sometimes he reached out of his quietness and flung a stone into the sea. In a kindly way. As you would touch a cat between times, for release. Away on the horizon a small trawler moved, passing on towards the fishing-grounds. The sea between, sparkling like points of schist. But he felt empty, old, alone. The day was a sealed aluminium can and he could not prise it open.

A rat appeared from between the rocks close to where he sat. It rooted among the jetsam, the seaweeds, the dirty, salt-sodden bits of timber and plastic. It was big. Patcho sat still as a stone. The rat sensed a presence and looked up at him. For a long moment they watched each other, united for a while in their foraging for consolation. The rat turned and busied itself, warily, at a distance. Patcho's instinct was to reach for a rock. No, he thought, no. We have damaged each other quite enough.

To his left, and suddenly, a small stone clattered along the rocks and died before it reached the sea. Patcho was startled. The rat vanished at once. Patcho saw a boy appear after the stone, rooting along the rocks and boulders. Patcho watched him. As he came closer the broken man saw at once that the boy had been crying; there was a little mucous still under his nose, his face was red and blotched. The boy picked up another stone and flung it with obvious anger against the sea. Then he saw Patcho Whelehan. Like man and rat, they watched each other for a while. Patcho did not stir. At last the boy began to move towards him, half cautiously, half indifferently. He stood a small distance behind Patcho, his shoe kicking at a barnacle on a rock. Patcho turned away, back towards the sea. Then he picked a can from the detritus near him and threw it out into the water. It floated, a small red adventurer on the high seas. Patcho stood up, gathered a fistful of stones, flung one at the can, and missed.

'Damn!' he said aloud, 'the pirates are making for the coast.'

His words came out from the side of his mouth, injured words, like small birds with damaged wings. He threw another stone, and missed again. Then he looked quickly over his shoulder.

'Help!' he called, 'they'll come screaming up the beach and kill us all.'

At once the boy had a stone in his hand. He flung it, wildly, and the stone splashed away into the sea. Patcho flung one that landed a little beyond the can, the waves bringing it closer to the shore. The boy threw again and almost hit the can and the splash filled it with water and it sank.

'Great shot!' Patcho cheered.

So they met, Patcho Whelehan and Paschal Sweeney, and sat a while quietly together on the low rocks at the edge of the Atlantic Ocean. For a time they flung stones, as far out as they could, circling one another. Paschal sniffed.

'Trouble at home?' Patcho guessed.

'Naw,' the boy said. 'It's Tim Nulty's gang. We're playing cowboys and Indians and I don't want to be an Indian. They always get killed. Tim is always the cowboy and he always wins.'

'So you told him . . . ?'

'I told him I want to win, sometimes, too – like, there must have been some good Indians!'

Patcho was silent for a while. Then he told the boy about Taras Bulba and his Cossacks, about his sons Ostap and Andrii, about the honour and bravery that were their creed; he told him of the great wide steppes of Russia and how the horses galloped across the plains, fast as the winds. He told him of the freedom of the Cossacks, how they drank and sang and fought. He told him of the wicked ways of the Tatars, and how the wild and wonderful Cossacks bore down on them at every opportunity. Sometimes winning. Sometimes losing. How Taras Bulba, leader and hero, was at last captured, crucified, and burned to death.

The young boy listened, enthralled, and the tide rose slowly till it almost touched their feet, and then it paused, and began to turn. Patcho's words, edged with spittle and slowed with effort, brought the young boy's mouth open with wonder, the eyes widened, the body stilled.

'Where did you hear all of that?' Paschal asked.

'I read a lot, in my den, because I'm alone a lot, you know; people don't like to be near a man like me because of my scars, my ugliness, and because of my job, too.'

The young boy, innocent still of real pain, looked up at him.

'I was told about your accident,' he said. He paused then, looked down at his feet. 'I don't think you're ugly,' he said.

Patcho smiled quietly to himself. They were silent for a while.

'What's your job, anyway?' Paschal asked him.

'I'm the coffin maker,' Patcho said. 'The whole third floor of MacHenry's General Store is mine. I live there. And I work there. And I read there and I sleep there. I have my books, my timber, my tools, there in my den. Would you like to see it?'

★

The top floor of MacHenry's General Store was wholly given over to the making of coffins. The outhouses were filled with timber, the planks and boards and plywoods that would be hoisted up by Patcho's own ingenious system of ropes and pulleys, to the door high in the gable wall. Aluminium bins, large and businesslike aluminium wheelbarrows, dinky green barrows with red wheels, the spades, shovels, scythes, the tins of paint, coils of barbed wire, chicken wire, stakes, oars, outboard engines – if MacHenry's General Store didn't have it, then it was not to be had on the island. In the yard there were two petrol pumps. The shop itself sold the lovely, old-fashioned linen nappies with their attendant, outsize safety pins and it sold, too, the latest in the disposable line. And everything else that brings a life from linen nappy to linen shroud.

The demand for coffins was a steady one, the sea being the sea and the islanders being islanders, not willing to waste valuable fishing time learning to swim, knowing in any case that the rains are persistent and the winds rise suddenly and unpredictably out at sea and that a man's life in the ocean is not worth a bubble, whether he can swim or no.

The loft was low and raftered like the island chapel. Patcho presiding. The MacHenrys left him alone. He had a phone up there and he could talk to the offices downstairs from where the customers could call him up without having to face him, without having to go out the back door of the shop, up the iron steps that clung like ivy to the gable wall, and in the wooden door at the top; they could leave all else to his discretion.

'Patcho.'

'Yes?'

'It's Callum, Patcho. I've Mrs Gillespie with me. Poor Anthony is after dyin' on her. Poor Anthony. Poor Mrs Gillespie.'

'Anthony the Gate Gillespie.'

'Yes, Patcho. Anthony the Gate.'

'Five feet ten or so. Give or take. Price range, Mr MacHenry?'

There was a whisper and a shuffling sound, someone's hand over the mouthpiece in the office.

'Middle range, Patcho. Middle range.'

'I'll have the coffin to the house by supper time.'

'Good man, Patcho. I'll tell...' but Patcho would already be at work.

The door in the gable wall, at the top of the iron steps, and under the pulley-and-rope contraption Patcho had erected, was a big wooden door that opened out over a salt field ending in rocks and the wild ocean. Patcho hoisted his timbers and lowered his coffins while, often, the storms sweeping down out of Iceland or rushing over from Newfoundland chewed at the wood and ruffled his thin, greying hair. He hoisted his supplies, his tea, his milk and sugar, his dinner that Mrs MacHenry cooked for him every day, his tobacco, his matches, his books... so that he never had need to come down and walk the earth amongst ordinary men.

It was not that Patcho Whelehan did not like ordinary people, but that he knew for a fact that ordinary people were not able for him. He lived now inside a body that was not acceptable to people who did not pause to think whether a thistle was a marvel of God's creation or a lamentable weed. The sky weighed down on Patcho's shoulders. If the beautiful things of the universe, he believed, reflect the absolute beauty of their Creator, then ordinary people thought that Patcho Whelehan reflected Satan. And ordinary people were not allowed enter the great loft where Satan worked, lived, ate, drank, slept, read and dreamed now more than he had ever dreamed before.

'You can do anything with pulleys,' Patcho told the boy as he led him in through the high door in the gable wall. 'You can lift the world onto your shoulders if you have pulleys. Watch.'

He pushed a coffin that stood on black trestles near the doorway over towards the wall. He opened the door onto the winds and the ocean. The coffin rested, like a diver, on the edge of the world. Patcho tied ropes around it, quickly, with the expert hands of a tar before the mast. Then he drew in one of the ropes that were positioned outside the gable door and fixed it to the ropes about the coffin. He winked at Paschal, gave a quick tug and the coffin sailed out on to the ocean of air. The boy gasped. Then the coffin sank, gently, like a feather, towards the earth. Patcho's hands working on the ropes.

'Your wood is a lovely creature,' Patcho said. 'A fine lover. It does what you ask of it, it takes the shape you want it to take. It is obedient, completely obedient, to your every whim, your every little will. The way a man should be before his Maker. And if God loves the creature that lets itself relax under God's shaping fingers, so I love this wood, I love it, as I try to love my own Maker. The Master. The real Master. The Crucified Christ Himself.' He chuckled.

Paschal leaned out from the opened door, carefully holding to one jamb. The coffin lay, perfectly still and safe, on the ground of the store yard. 'If I get into it,' he said impulsively, 'can you pull it back up?'

Patcho's eyes brightened. 'Good lad, good lad,' he laughed. 'I like to see a bit of magic in your thoughts.'

Paschal scurried down the iron steps and sat into the coffin, holding the sides as he would the gunwales of a boat. 'Right!' he shouted. 'I'm an Indian and I need to get in over the high walls of the fort!'

Instantly the coffin began to rise, yawing sickeningly till

Paschal got his weight correctly placed. Then Patcho pulled more strongly. Paschal heard the smooth sounds of the ropes moving through the pulleys, a gentle sound, like the tongue of an animal on its own flank. He rose, majestically, the world dropping away around him, the hedgerows, the fields, even the sea falling off to the coffin master's power. For a moment the coffin hung suspended, fifty feet in the air, just outside the open door. Then Patcho chuckled again, pulled on another rope and the coffin with its young donkey-boy aboard sailed smoothly in to land.

'Wow!' Paschal said, and Patcho laughed at the face before him, wide with delight and astonishment.

'Up here,' Patcho said as he untied the ropes, 'it's my own world now. I have only to deal with the timber, ash, elm, oak, teak, beautiful, gentle creatures. Cedar. Walnut. Mahogany. Birch. Timber is a gift of God's, boy, a great gift and so it is despised. But I love it, pith, sap and heartwood. I had a gun, Paschal, once, a shotgun, its stock was walnut and even then I loved to touch it, caress it, love it. And now I have my whole list of friends to help me, chisels, planes, coping saw, ripsaw, my drills and bits, my braces and augers, my assistants, my friends, my lovers.'

Patcho's hand was sweeping grandly round the walls. Everywhere, cartridge-belts were fastened to the walls and, in-stead of cartridges, the tools stood proud and gleaming in the pouches.

'You have to make amends, you know, for the wrongs you do the world.' Patcho's voice was low now, and grave. 'You have to make amends. You have to get the balance right. Re-store the equilibrium. Between yourself and nature. Between yourself and man. Between man and God. And I am a sinner, Paschal, we are all sinners, but I'm the greatest sinner of them all. My work restores the balance. Up here I take the world I used to break in pieces and I create these things of beauty, these, my coffins. They are doors, boy, doors the people must one day knock on, to be admitted to another world. Where everything that has been unequal will be made equal. Where everything that was unbalanced will be put right.'

The man, limping, his misshapen hand gesticulating with pride and decision, knocked on the coffin lids as they stood, silent as sentries, about the walls. 'Knock, knock,' he said, listening after. 'Knock, knock. Who's there? Me. It's me. Patrick Joseph Whelehan. I'm tired of this selfish, greedy world. Can I come in where there's no more tears, or pain, or suffering?' He put his ear to the coffin lid. 'Have I earned my invitation? Look at me! I'm crucified. My face. My hands. My legs. I know what pain is. I know suffering. I know death. Because I knocked, loudly, but I wasn't ready yet, there was no equilibrium in me . . .'

He listened again. Then his face lit up dramatically. 'I can come in!' he announced. 'I can open the door of death and I can pass right in.'

He laughed. The boy stood, intrigued, barely understanding, watching. The coffins were in neat rows along the loft, some almost finished, resting on low trestles, others on a workbench, naked, white, as if shivering. The smell of wood and varnish was pervasive and pleasant. Wood shavings everywhere. Paschal walked through a whispering, soft-spoken underworld.

'I am free up here,' Patcho went on eagerly as if he had not spoken to anyone for a long long time. 'Free. I have to deal only with wood, and with my tools. When you deal with men you are debased, you come to depend on them, for friendship, for food, for laughter, for love. And they will let you down, be sure of it, they will let you down. But here, I am slave to no man, I am free. Rely only on yourself, young lad, on nature, and on God. For as soon as you begin to rely on other men so soon are you a slave, and all the balance in your life will slip away.'

Patcho ran his hand with affection along the naked, white shoulder of a coffin. Then he stopped. He turned quickly to the boy, winked and beckoned. 'Here, Paschal,' he said, moving towards a dim corner of the loft. 'Here. My own, special doorway to God's care.'

The boy saw a coffin, finished, polished, accoutred with all the fittings and brasses imaginable. Patcho touched it, lovingly. He walked slowly round it, his broken hand soothing it. He looked deeply contented. And at peace.

'I lie in this coffin sometimes,' he said, 'and dream.'

He climbed on to the trestle and lay down carefully in the coffin. He folded his hands over his chest. He closed his eyes.

'Here I can be anyone,' he said, ecstatically. 'I can be Taras Bulba on a great white stallion, pursuing villains across the steppes. I can be the ancient mariner, alone on a great ghost ship, silent on a silent ocean.' He opened his eyes suddenly, and looked at Paschal. 'Or I can be Patrick Joseph Whelehan, flying like an eagle through summer skies, flying higher and higher, up to the threshold of heaven itself. And then I can raise my hands and knock and God will let me in. To Paradise. Through that door there, Paschal, that door there.'

Against the wall stood a coffin lid, polished, finished, carrying the gleaming brass plate. On it was inscribed:

PATRICK JOSEPH WHELEHAN
Died into the arms of God
Rest in Peace

Patcho left the loft sometimes and walked in the late evenings, sometimes when the stars shone and sea and sky seemed merged to one. He walked at times, and in places, where he could be almost certain he would not meet any man, woman or child. He walked now, more content in himself, now that he had a friend, a young boy innocent and hurt and willing to be free.

Patcho walked, without his guns, across the high reaches of the mountain where he had slaughtered pheasant, grouse, wild goat, where he had gouged wounds in the flesh of nature. The night was calm and still. The stars were a fine patterning of brightness and miracle and if you could reach out from here you could bathe your being in their light. Space, he thought, space and time and all the great pulleys and mechanisms that name the universe both separate us from God, He is so vast, so far away from us, and draws us, near to Him, near to His beauty, His power, His glory, all at the same time.

Somewhere on the mountainside he could hear the ugly, intrusive sounds of an engine. Vaguely, far below, he saw headlights shifting dimly upwards. The sound was alien to the night. The jerky, turning lights seemed to Patcho like crude, probing fingers. The vehicle was working its way slowly up the rough-stone road towards Julia Wrynne's house. There was nothing else up there. Patcho stopped to watch. Below him the island lay sleeping like a large black animal stretched out at its owner's feet. The vehicle stopped somewhere down along the mountainside. Silence came like a high wave up along the heathers and hillocks. The lights had been switched off. Patcho began to feel anxious. The doctor? perhaps Julia was ill? the priest? But he had known that the sound of the engine was unfamiliar, raucous, no bringer of release. He began to move slowly and slantwise along the side of the mountain.

Soon he heard the engine start up again, he saw the lights switched on, the vehicle roared violently, shattering the night like a pane of glass. The vehicle seemed to lurch and veer back down the road in a great hurry. Patcho watched it. He could see the tiny red tail-lights, he could see how the headlights picked out an occasional whin bush or a lone fuchsia-tree, a boulder, the rough-stone road. He watched it as it reached the road below. It turned right, and he could still hear and see it as it sped towards the northern end of the island. Slowly the sounds faded away and then he could no longer see the lights. He hurried towards the old woman's cottage.

They had taken the van to the very edge of the island, up the high road that petered out along the cliff-top. There was a wide, grassy space and beyond it the rough shingle and sand cart-track led steeply on down into a quiet bay. It was the world's rim; far below the ocean idled under the stars; distance and space and time, no more.

'They'll not find th' oul' bitch for days,' Kane said, sitting in the driver's seat of the van. 'We'll do a few likelier-lookin' spots the morrow an' get the fuck off this island!'

Madden peered forward through the dirty windscreen.

'It's awful quiet up here,' he said, and shivered. 'It's the fuckin' middle of the back of no place.'

Kane grunted. He heaved himself out of the van and slammed the door shut. The sound sent a shiver across the night. Cautiously he walked to the grassy edge of the cliff and peered over.

'Fuck!' he said, stepping back quickly. Then he opened the fly of his trousers and pissed out into the emptiness. He looked around. There was no house within miles, no lights, no sheds, just this half-road that faded away to a track that led on down into darkness. 'Fuck!' he said again. A sheep bleated somewhere far down below him.

Madden got out his side of the van and banged his door

shut. He came and stood by Kane, opened his fly and pissed onto the grass edge. 'Fuckin' horrible lonesome up here, Kane!'

'Shut up! It's bad enough without you moanin' about it.'

Madden did up his fly. He moved around the van. The starlight made the world bright with a faint, mercurial beauty. Madden gathered a large white stone from near the cliff-edge and placed it in front of the wheel of the van. Then he stood back. Kane was watching him.

'I'll not sleep a fuckin' wink up in this wilderness,' he complained.

'Scared of ghosts?'

Madden grunted. He opened the back door of the van. There were two mattresses on the floor, with dirty blankets flung on top of them. He climbed in.

'Take your fuckin' boots off!' Kane muttered. 'I don't want you kickin' me as well as snorin' your head off all night.'

They left their boots under the back of the van. Both men slept almost at once, the back door of the van closed over. There was silence. The sea far below was gentle, stirring almost inaudibly under the stars. Here and there a sheep moved about the slopes, its white shape soft against the darkness. The world went on turning, slowly, as if there were nothing but peace.

Pat Joe Whelehan's stunted shape materialised out of the darkness. He moved with almost total silence, scarcely seeming to breathe. He stood a long while at the edge of the road watching the dark shape of the van. Then he moved forward, stealthily. He stood at the back of the van, listening to the sounds of heavy breathing from within. Cautiously he moved around the van and stood watching out over the cliff to the great spaces of sea and sky. Then he sighed deeply. He moved the big stone away from the front wheel. Then, with infinite caution, he opened the door on the driver's side. There was a slight, irritated squeaking from the door's hinges. The loud breathing of the men in the van did not alter. Patcho released the handbrake on the van, reached over and drew the gear lever into neutral. He took the driving wheel and turned it, slowly, until the front wheels pointed towards the long slope of the dirt-track that led away into the darkness of the bay far, far below. Then he went to the back of the van, leaned against it, and heaved.

Very, very slowly the van moved, giving a long soft sigh of effort. Patcho stood back. The van moved gently, mincingly almost, the wheels on the gravel speaking their low words of regret. Then it gathered speed as it began down the slope. It went completely silent for a while over the salt grass by the edge of the cliff. Patcho could see the angle narrowing and suddenly the van veered out over the cliff-ledge. There was a moment of total silence and then Patcho heard the van smashing onto rocks somewhere down the cliff-face. There was a great rending of metal and a sudden gush of flames, followed quickly by a great splash as the van was swallowed up in the sea below. Silence settled back almost at once, only the gentle sorrowing sound of the ocean coming up from the depths. Patcho turned away. Two pairs of worn boots stood forlornly on the gravel.

Where he stood, catching his breath, high over the fields, Paschal shuddered as if he were cold. He began to hurry. He had to be at Granny Julia's cottage before noon. In the distance he could see the squat louvred belfry of the island church. It would peal out at noon. 'The angel of the Lord...' and he had such things to do.

They thought, the adults, that it was all so neat, so ordered. They were certain of it! The darkness that stood tall in the central crossroads of their lives, their very own, dreaded, frightening coffin master had at last shown what he was made of! Hadn't he killed, brutally, the one innocent person this island really knew? That was what they were saying, all of them, because that's what every child in the school was saying. Paschal alone had stayed silent, dismayed, hurt, lost. Incredulous. And then the fire, that awful, overwhelming fire, sent by God, they said, as a punishment on the coffin master, symbol of the fires of hell that awaited his black, distorted, soul. They were so smug, so satisfied! And they had seen him, the people had witnessed it, that misshapen figure caught on the high reaches of the house while the fire raged around him. They had seen him wave, they knew he must have been screaming for help and his screams were drowned by the triumphant cries of the fire. He had been swallowed to ash by the anger of God and justice had been done!

Paschal hurried on. The ground was soft and springy where the mosses grew, but here and there were soft, wet places where a boy could sink to his waist. As he rose higher a light breeze began to reach around the shoulder of the mountain and he relished it, raising his hot face to its comfort. There were sheep scattered over the commonage, their wool deeply marked with dyes to distinguish them for their owners. Their heavy black heads lifted from their chewing to watch the young boy as he jumped and ran.

Paschal had come several times during the last few days to the blackened space that had been MacHenry's General Store. He had stood, silenced, before that awful absence. He shuddered at the memory of the fire, how painful it must be to be burned to death. He had stood a long time and had come away, deeply unhappy. One afternoon he had climbed again to Julia Wrynne's house. Alone, because now none of the adults approached the place, nor did the boys go near the mountainside in their play. Only the ghosts shifted there in patches of sunlight or sighed heavily on the breeze.

He had been scared. The house stood, as it had always stood, the door shut, the windows dark and curtainless. He half-expected to see the door open and Granny Julia coming out, rubbing her hands in her apron, a big welcoming smile on her face. He had circled the old house, his small being flooded with loss and sorrow. The back of the house had weeds already beginning to push through the cracked stonework of the yard. Granny Julia used to throw kettles of scalding water about that yard. And he had often seen her stoop to root out a dandelion, or a nettle, or a clump of grass. Idly he scuffed the toe of his shoe against a stone. When he heard his name called softly from behind him he screamed with terror. Patcho Whelehan stood in the doorway of the old shed. He stood, smiling his crooked, gentle smile, his hands by his side, his clothes ragged and stained.

He said Paschal's name again. 'How are you, son?' he said.

The boy could not move.

'But . . . you're, you're dead. I saw you . . .'

Patcho laughed. He hit the jamb of the old door with his damaged hand.

'Not dead, son, no,' he laughed, 'not dead yet!'

He stepped out into the sunlight at the edge of the yard. For a moment Paschal felt he wanted to turn and run, screaming, back down the road towards the village. But he had known Patcho, his kindliness, his gentle, hurt ways. And gathering all his young life into the movement he stepped forward to meet the ghost. Quickly they embraced, the old man clasping the boy tightly to him. Paschal knew the solidity of that flesh, the familiar fusty smell of the man's clothes, the strength in the arms.

'Affliction is a strange friend,' Patcho said. 'It makes you do all sorts of things. They killed poor Julia, killed her for no reason at all and that could not be left unpunished. There was something terrible and unfinished about that night, Paschal. The balance of the world had been awry. The equilibrium. The truth.'

He told him about the van, how he had found her killers, what he had done. 'I know that was wrong, too, Paschal,' he said. They sat together on the low wall of the yard. 'But there was more than justice. Julia and I were close. Poor Julia. She was fond of me, always fond of me, and when I had my accident and looked so terrible she grew even more fond of me. And I of her. We were good, close friends, boy, and I knew for sure I was the only one who could give her rest at last.'

Patcho paused, glancing at the old yard.

'Now there's one more thing has to be balanced up,' he said. 'I knew they'd think I killed poor Julia, I knew they'd be wanting to think that. Because people are fools, blind, stupid fools without imagination. They'll always play cowboys and Indians and the cowboys will always win. Always. So I knew they'd think I killed her. They'd try to put me in gaol, Paschal, and I couldn't take that. That's not the way things are made even again. So I bought myself some time. I took what I needed from the store and brought it up here. After they took poor Julia away. I knew Julia was at peace then, that she had begun to float into that great emptiness that is fuller than all the world. In the coffin I made for her. Poor Julia, poor Julia Wrynne.'

He stopped again. He picked up a pebble in his wasted hand. Paschal saw the stumps of his fingers, how he took the pebble between thumb and little finger. The boy wondered how it would have been possible to live with a hand like that.

Patcho seemed to know what he was thinking and he laughed, chucking the pebble idly across the yard. 'Looks ugly, doesn't it?' he said. 'But I know it was this hand, and my torn

face, that helped me become a different person. Detached.
There's a word, son. Detached. Not tied down. Not tied down
by power, or wealth, or even love. Free. As Jesus Christ was
free. Except that he, too, had a job to do.'

Patcho told the boy that he had climbed back into
MacHenry's Store one night and waited. How he had set fire,
then, to the wood-shavings in the shop. How he had made a
great noise to wake the sleeping family below.

'They got out. I knew they'd get out. And I wanted to finish
all that work up there, all those coffins, and screws, and
plaques. I thought only the workshop would burn up. Because
it was on the top of the house. But the place had too much
timber, too much dry wood, too many shavings, too many
coffins. And the floor began to burn. Then it collapsed and
the fire just went down into the rooms below. I could have
died, then, I really could. But I didn't want it that way,
Paschal, without anybody knowing the truth. I wanted to let
the people know what they had done to me and to Julia, ostracising her, ostracising me, abandoning us because we were of
the poor, the suffering poor. The only friend was you, Paschal,
you're the first person ever seemed to care about Julia, and
about me. She spoke about you, you're true, boy, true. And
I'll need your help in what I have to do.'

He paused a long time, watching away along the slopes of
the mountain.

'Anyway, when I saw all the people gathered outside the
burning house, I set up a great yelling and screeching and waving of arms so they'd all see me for sure. And then I slipped
away, swung out the gable door on my ropes and pulleys and
slipped into the darkness along the shore. I was just in time, for
the whole house collapsed shortly after. I've been up here ever
since, waiting. Praying, too. For what I have to do will not be
easy. And I knew you'd come soon. For Julia would call you.

And I could trust you. Because I'll need you, Paschal, son, I'll depend on you to make my plan work before the eyes of all the people.'

Now Paschal was approaching the house from the slopes of the mountain. He was not quite sure he'd be able to carry out Patcho's wishes. But he would have to try. Patcho had spoken to him of Christ, in words much more real than Miss Tighe had ever used, or Father Muldoon, either. How this man had worked for the people, giving himself to them, how they had thrown him out, rejected him, because he had shown them that all their worldly goods and all their power would avail them nothing, because they would have to leave all that and die. He showed them the truth. He was their coffin master and look what they did to him! And what they have been doing all down the centuries. To the innocent, the hurt, the true!

Paschal watched the house for a while. He scanned the road and the fields below. There was no sign of life. No movement. He left the hillock and crossed Julia's front yard. Then he stopped again, at the angle of the house, suddenly terrified of what he would find, of what he would have to do. He had never felt so alone in his life, so helpless, so unsure.

Patcho Whelehan had brought with him two large, finely planed beams of cedar wood. He had dug a hole in the centre of Julia Wrynne's back yard, lifting away the stones. He had cut the timber beams to a special size and nailed one across the other. Then he laid the beams on the yard, the base balanced by the edge of the hole. He fixed a series of ropes and pulleys to the chimney of Julia's house on one side, the roof of the shed on the other. He pulled gently on one of the ropes and the cross dropped into the hole and rose steadily till it was standing upright. Patcho lowered the cross again with a sigh of satisfaction.

He spent all of that Friday morning in Julia Wrynne's room, talking with her, praying. Late in the morning he took off his clothes and wrapped himself only in a small linen cloth. He fixed a vice to a piece of timber on the left beam of the cross. He fixed another to the end of the right beam. He had his hammer. He had sharp, four-inch nails.

Only once did Patcho pause in his labours. He looked up at the clear blue sky over the island. Only a few small clouds moved up there. He could hear a mountain pipit sing its jerky song somewhere, the occasional scolding call of a wheatear. Far away up the mountainside he heard the high-pitched predatory whistle of a hawk. He looked back once to the windows of Julia's house. They were eyes, blinded and dark. For a moment he saw her again, lifting that squeaking back-door latch, stepping out into the yard, humming some tuneless song, scattering water from a basin out over the stones. He saw her stop, letting the basin hang heavy in her left hand, saw the rest of the water drip lazily by her feet, her big red hand move slowly to push back the hair from her forehead. He heard her say his name, just once, whispering it behind a broad, cheerful smile. Then she turned from him and went back inside, the latch dropping into place with a dull, iron *amen*.

Patcho stretched himself out carefully on the cross. He tied a rope tightly about his legs, just above his knees. He tied another, loosely, around the wood under the place his chest would be. He left the ends of that rope ready. For Paschal, should he come. Then he put his left hand down on the beam. It fitted perfectly in under the open teeth of the vice. He took one of the shining nails and fitted that into the vice so that it hovered an inch above the timber. He tightened the vice to allow the lightest of grips on the nail. Then he did the same with the vice on the right-hand beam. Above this one he had carefully suspended an iron weight; when he struck the nail on the left-hand side it would release a smaller system of ropes and pulleys, allowing thirty seconds to get his right hand back in under this second vice. The iron would descend. It would do. For a moment Patcho lay back on the cross. He closed his eyes. The boy would be along soon. He believed that. Poor Paschal. It would be difficult for him. But he would come through. Patcho needed him, to finish his work, to be a witness, to be an Easter for him before the people.

He sat up again, measuring his length along the beam. Then he nailed a block of wood at a careful distance from the base, testing it for firmness. He was ready. It would hold.

Pat Joe Whelehan stretched his miserable left hand carefully until the palm of it lay under the point of the nail in the vice. He gripped the hammer tightly in his right hand.

'Forgive me, Julia,' he said aloud. 'Forgive me, Paschal. Forgive me, Christ.'

He raised the hammer high.

BETWEEN TIMES

It was a cancer in him. He had always known it somehow, but had never allowed the thought to stay for long on the surface of his consciousness. He had imagined it as the tiny tuber of an orchid, lying dormant in the seasoning flesh of his body, small and tight and self-contained. Waiting. Until something stirred in the dank earth of his being and the bulb split open, slowly, the first soft shoots beginning to reach upwards through his clay. And eventually the great wound of the flower, blood-purple, became manifest in his life.

'Let's just change into our pyjamas there, like a good man, climb into bed and we'll be back to you in a minute.'

He stood, disturbed, behind the big, pastel-flowered hospital screen. *Our* pyjamas! Treating him now like a child were they, trusting him to do what he was bidden so they could show approval?

He undressed with difficulty, breathing heavily, the body slow and responding only with reluctance. He left his clothes at the foot of the bed. Folded neatly, as usual. He could hear shuffling and murmuring outside the flowered plastic curtains. He drew on the new pyjamas that had been perfectly folded; they were fresh and caressed his body with their comfort. He drew back the triangle of blanket and sheet and climbed into bed.

This was the moment he had been anticipating all his life, one he had glimpsed at unexpected moments, looking up from his desk to greet a friend, or turning from admiring a bluebell in a wood, and he would feel the great, insistent pressure of this very instant, a sense of cream-coloured walls, of antiseptic smells, of white ceilings, as he climbed for the last time into a bed. Climbed – for it was high, the metal bars rising behind the heaped pillows, climbed – onto a scaffold, a raft, onto his mother's knee.

'You can come!' He grumbled the words when he had settled himself against the pillows in the bed.

The nurse came through the curtains at once, clucking, big-bosomed, buttoned and starched. 'There we are then! Good man. We'll just take away these things, till we need them again.'

We! Indeed. *Need them again!* Not likely. Soon they'll be lift-ing bars up around my bed, keeping me in a cot the way you keep a baby. He sniffled and looked away as she picked up his big underpants, flicked them into the pile with the rest. She stooped, gathered his socks off the floor. He blushed: was, per-haps, becoming like a baby again, untidy, careless . . . She put his old suitcase on the bed and folded the clothes neatly, inside. She muttered betimes, like a hen in a farmyard under noon sunshine.

'Humph!' he offered. 'I expect you to lay an egg any minute.'

'There we are then!' – as she slapped the clothes tighter and brought down the lid of the suitcase. 'I'll put this out in the lockers, all ready for when you'll be going home.'

For a moment he was grateful to her for the lie. Going home. True, in a way, for he was going home, but the leather suitcase would not be needed, nor suit, nor underpants, nor socks. He could say goodbye to that suitcase, had been with him in hotel rooms about the world, Paris, Madeira, Mauritius, America... He watched it eagerly now, the dunts and scrapes where the old leather showed its flesh. The nurse put his shoes on top of it, lifted it against her chest, grinned at him and disappeared, like a well-rehearsed actress, through the curtains.

He remembered standing in breathtaking sunshine at the edge of a field of sunflowers somewhere in Umbria, light hovering in noon-stillness and heat, watching the high trail of a jet plane move soundlessly across the silver blue sky; he remembered the sudden weight of the suitcase he had just hauled down off a bus, remembered the homesickness he had known at that moment, his impatience to be gone, to be back among people and objects trusted and known; to be back with Ruth, home, safe, and loved. How foolish we are, he thought, hastening always to be anywhere other than where we are, to have time leap by so we can touch again on familiar ground. How he wished now he could have that moment back, to savour it, to slow time down, to hold and caress the day the way the landscape of Italy had tried to hold and embrace his big body. He had been sullen and irritable. Now he sighed and closed his eyes. He was weary.

They would poke and prod him, test, prescribe, encourage. He would submit, because these were the conventions. They would stand, white-coated wonderboys, at the foot of the bed, consulting with one another, one hand in the pocket, and he would watch their ties, the rings on their fingers, the precise striped trousers showing underneath the clinical whites. He would nod at their words of wisdom, their findings, he would stroke their pride and listen while they purred like slow tom-cats. They could probe and search, with their fine instruments, with their machetes, but they could not ever root out the great wound of his mortality. Or of their own, for that matter. He would be even more amused when the big chief came, the others about him like lambs after mother sheep. Passing in a cloud of glory. Tossing a few big words behind him, like droppings.

Nurse Cummings was her name. She was gentle with him, though he could imagine her wrestling sacks of potatoes up onto the backs of trailers. She busied herself about him, straightening the sheets, arranging the flowers on his bedside table, comforting his pillows.

'You're like a mother goose,' he offered.

She slapped the blankets into perfect surfaces. She smiled at him, like an indulgent granny.

'They gave me a book, sister,' he went on.

'Nurse,' she replied, 'I'm only a nurse. Nurse Cummings. Not sister. Not sister anything.'

'Not yet, anyway.'

'No chance ever, with my reputation!'

'They gave me a book, sister. I'll call you sister, if you don't mind. You're a good nurse.'

'You're a charmer, Mr Dunne. Now if the both of us was just that wee bit younger ...'

'If we were, sister, if we were, we'd be lying in a field of daisies.'

'Not with our weather, Mr Dunne, we wouldn't.'

'They gave me this book, Sister Cummings. *A Suitable Boy,* it's called. More than a thousand pages in it. More than a thousand. I won't even begin it. You can have it.'

'Oh you should give it a try, Mr Dunne.' Cheerily.

He smiled up at her; he said nothing. He was still handsome, she thought, when he smiled.

'Will you marry me, Sister Death?' he said suddenly, through his smile.

★

When Ruth came at visiting time his life filled up with tender-
ness and sorrow. He was happiest when no one else intruded,
no matter how well-intentioned they might be. How strange
that it was only now they could find space together, she sitting
at the side of the hospital bed, holding his hand, their eyes on
one another. And all the years behind them had been cramped
and loud with busyness and interruptions. He would trade the
world now, trade house, lands, if only . . . And he stopped the
thought. It was a skylark soaring away into impossible
sunlight.

Sometimes she brought him glucose drinks, and sometimes
grapes. She always ensured there were flowers for the small
glass vase. She brought him whiskey, too, filling the hip-flask
he kept in a deep pocket of his dressing gown. It mellowed
him, in the sand-blown, ice-cold wilderness before night, he
would swirl it slowly round in his mouth and think of her
kisses, the asking fire of her loving. He knew these were grace
days, gifted to him. For some purpose.

Ruth was with him the afternoon when something snapped
and the questioning began. He said a word out loud, mumbled
it rather, and she asked him: 'What did you say?'

He looked blankly at her and for a moment he could not
name her. And then he remembered, he squeezed her hand
and said it: 'Ruth!' he said, 'Ruth, Ruth, Ruth.'

Something ferocious struck him from within where the
orchid was in full bloom, some vicious frosting, some harsh,
fathomless cut. He gasped and sat up violently in the bed.
Ruth was alarmed and stood to reach for the bell-push. He
could see her move towards it, dread and terror on her face,
her long fingers reaching.

But he had stepped away from her, out through a thick curtain of gauze, bits and strips of gossamer clinging to him that
he tried to wipe away. He felt well again and strong, but he

was no fool. He knew. It was a landscape like (where was it?) Umbria, the same dry heat, the same silver blue sky, the same hills, an ochre landscape, without life. On the summit of one distant hill he could see a town, a high red campanile, the brown stone tiles of roofs, the yellow-brown old-city walls. He began walking. There was no road. Just a dusty-dun earth, crusted and hot.

His feet were bare and the hot clay just tolerable. But he was elated, hadn't he always known there was something? and here he was, proud to have come through. Smug. Bringing his wisdom with him. Not once did he look back to see where he had come from. If only Ruth were with him now!

He stopped. There was a scorpion on the ground in front of him. Of all things in the world he hated and feared the scorpion. He shuddered. Its body was long and black; its pincers and that awful, upcurled, turned-back tail with its deadly agony-inducing sting, were flesh-coloured. The colour of pus. He was conscious of the vulnerability of his naked feet. He shifted to the right. To go round it. Cautiously. Tiptoeing. And there was another one. And another! And yet more! Motionless. Small black lumps of vicious hatred. He knew at once there would be thousands of them. Millions. He shivered violently. Trying not to make a sudden movement, he lifted his head and scanned the landscape. Umbria. *Sister Mother Earth*. And like sharp pebbles along a disappointing strand, the scorpions were everywhere. Poised, and waiting.

He took a step. Nothing happened. Another. His feet were on the hot earth. His bare flesh almost touching the creatures. He decided again. Began to walk, lifting his eyes towards the hills. At once a scorpion darted at his right foot and he screamed with the intensity of the pain. He closed his eyes to a purple light of agony and when he opened them Ruth was there, stretching her hand out towards the bell. He was sweating and breathless. She held his arm, shushing him. He laid his head against her breast and she fondled him, softly, like a child.

He rested against her a long, long time. There were no words. Her touch, the scent of her living, comforted and eased him. The pain in his chest was a great ache but there was release as he lay against her. He drew each breath in from a very long distance, forced it down into his lungs and heaved and hauled it out again. Sister Cummings was with him, rolling up his pyjama sleeve; there was a tiny sting and almost at once he could feel light and gentle warmth spread through him. He raised his eyes to her and tried to smile. She soothed him with mothering, sibilant sounds.

'Sister... Death,' he whispered but they could not understand his words.

He closed his eyes again, gratefully, and he was sliding down a long, dark chute, it was gentle, and when he came out on the other end he was not surprised to find himself in Umbria once more, the same landscape, filled now with vineyards, with fields of sunflowers, with trees. He could see no scorpions. There were birds singing.

He stood still for a long time, breathing in the good air. The sun stood hot and dazzling. Slowly he unbuttoned his shirt, the sleeves, the neck. If only there was somebody he could speak to. He called out, tentatively: 'Hello!'

There was no answer. At the edge of a wood nearby he saw a shed, the big door open. He moved, gratefully, towards its shade. He passed in. It was dark and cool. He moved forward, his hands stretched out in the blackness. The shed door swung shut behind him. It clicked to, with a firm, metallic sound. There was absolute darkness. He called out again, panic in his voice: 'Is there anybody here?'

His words echoed and fell back at his feet. The air was

growing hotter. The very silence about him seemed to burn. The cement floor under his naked feet was hot. He turned back towards the door but could not see the slightest thread of light. His hands touched a wall. It was too hot. He jerked back. The heat intensified. He took his vest off and rubbed his face with it. He stepped forward, a blind, naked, sweating animal, afraid and confused. And then the earth before him opened as if a trapdoor had swung away beneath him and he fell forward, screaming. His hands flailed wildly for hold and he gripped something, a beam, a bar, something. He was hanging from it, his body swaying out into emptiness. Dimly he could see a great chasm below, as if the shed straddled a vast cleft in the high reaches of a mountain. *Let go, let go!* The words echoed somewhere inside him. Far below there were boulders, a stream, trees. Tiny and distant and silent. The fall would shatter him into pieces. He held on, frantically, called out, it was her name he called, Ruth! Ruth! He held on, tightly. He opened his eyes.

She was watching down at him, tears in her eyes. His breathing was harsh, each breath an effort of the entire body. But he forced himself to smile up at her and he could see a distant, sad smile mirroring his. Sister Cummings was beside him, she was fastening a small, clear plastic mask on to his face. He struggled against it for a moment but then he could feel the oxygen reach him, his lungs relaxing, his body knowing some ease. He was grateful, tried to whisper, 'Sister . . . Death . . .' He knew no words had come out, perhaps a small dribble of saliva on his lips, because Ruth had stooped over him and was wiping his mouth, gently. He felt her hand in his and he tried to press it but it was no good, he was back in that dreaded shed with inhuman suddenness. He was naked, leaning out over that awful hole in the world's surface, holding with all his strength, holding someone's wrists, trying to heave someone back from that awful drop.

He knew he had been holding on for a very long time. Sweat poured from him. He strained, but could not heave that body up beside him. He looked down. Her face was gazing up at him, it was Ruth, young, beautiful, her body dangling out over the abyss. Her eyes pleaded with him, she opened her mouth but he could hear no words from her, just that old echo inside him, *let go, let go, let go*. He raised his eyes again to the darkness above him, pleading, begging for help. He held her, desperately, he could not, he would not let her go, never, ever, ever. He screamed, as loudly as he could, 'No! No! No! No! No!'

Someone spoke then, a kindly, vaguely familiar voice.

'Let's just change into our pyjamas there, like a good man, and climb into bed and we'll be back to you in a minute.'

He was standing, disturbed, behind a big, pastel-flowered hospital screen. He undressed, with difficulty. Breathing heavily, the body slow and responding only with reluctance. He left his clothes at the foot of the bed. Folded neatly, as usual. Then drew back the triangle of blanket and sheet and climbed into bed. Climbed – for it was high, the metal bars rising behind the heaped pillows, climbed – onto a scaffold, a raft, onto his mother's knee.

POSTE RESTANTE

One of the things I loved most was a hot whiskey after Sunday mass. It got the cold marble pillars out of me. It cleared away the Jesuit must. It spiced the beef. And it brought us closer together. Even for that one short hour of the week. Remember? But then came the peeling of the potatoes. I submitted to that, after the whiskey. How many potatoes does one peel in a lifetime? I wonder. I could ask somebody – now there I go again! *somebody!* language! I never do seem to get my words right, even here – I *could* ask, because it's all recorded. Still, it seems such a petty thing and there are so many other things to figure out. But however. Anyway. My poor hands were red and chapped from the potatoes, that much I know. And you! you never peeled a spud in your life! wouldn't know the difference between a spud and an egg! But however. None of that. It's all one now and I mustn't say a bad word about the living. *Nihil nisi bonum,* wasn't that it?

I have been making all sorts of signs and signals to you and you haven't responded to any of them. It's dispiriting. There's a word now! *Dis-spiriting.* That suits! Do you remember, just before you got up that morning, you stiffened? I could see you struggling with the weight of the day ahead. The door pushed open. Do you remember? I could see you, you were startled, naturally. You sensed something on the air. Well, the door opening like that, that was me.

It was, I suppose, a cry for help but it was already too late. I could see how distracted you grew, almost at once, because there must have been a strong smell. You did not hurry, oh no, you never hurried. You got up, lumberingly. You took the picture of the Crucified Christ from the dressing-table and you kissed it. You knelt on the frayed carpet by the bed and muttered. I could hear the words. They were only words, dear, useless, like pebbles flung against a black cloud keeping out the sun. You'd have been embarrassed if you knew I could hear you! we'd all be embarrassed if people knew the things we asked of Himself! Childish, silly, selfish things! Anyway. Your words were dust. And I was urging you, *hurry, hurry, hurry*, I was saying, *I'm in trouble, I need you, I need you, hurry!*

You hoisted yourself off your knees like a wounded soldier. I felt like chivvying you, *come on, don't be acting the martyr, you can't fool me*, shouting at you, *not any more you can't fool me, you never did fool me*, but I didn't say any of that because I felt sorry for you, there you were, you looked oh so old there, struggling off your knees after your sorry prayers, struggling to stand upright, and because I knew so well the sad condition of our kind, our hopes and dreams that slowly stiffen and rot away while the body grows heavy with its woe, grows old and ugly and pathetic. And, of course, I knew the awful grief you would have to shoulder soon, very, very soon. Since then, sometimes (what other word can I use except *sometimes?*), I have wondered whether I was adept at laying grief upon you, in order to lessen my own, and if this was a further attempt, the final attempt, to remonstrate with you, to make you accept my suffering and, therefore, my existence.

There now! I've always been a one for interrupting myself. Putting my words down and letting them run loose. Like earwigs shaken out of a dahlia flower. Anyway. Anyway. I had dragged myself off my knees too, a while earlier than you. I was still there, in the kitchen, still dressed in that old nightdress. I stood upright for a while, filled with the most extraordinary sense of wonder. And elation. You know that elation you get after the tablets have begun to work, that swing from depression to joy, a swing too far at first, too far, so that you used to say you dreaded my presence more when I was elated than when I was depressed? But I'm talking, love, about affliction now, not about depression, nor even pain; *affliction*, that's the word, a grief beyond naming.

Dearest, life is bitter. It has been so for us both. I have been trying to tell you... I telephoned the other day, I managed that, yes, I can do things like that. And you picked up the phone.

'Hello,' you said, and the word was a dull iron thud into the speaker.

I dropped my words into this end, softly, yet loud enough...

'Hello! hello! hello!' you said, loudly, angrily.

I tried again, a little more loudly, cautiously chosen words, forgiveness, understanding, love.

All you did was take the phone from your ear, look at it with hatred and slap it down again. I had not got through to you. I've tried, for your sake, not for my own. What I have been trying to tell you is simple, dearest; accept affliction, that's it, just accept it; fight it, of course, but then accept it. Without affliction we might so easily forget. And we had our share of affliction, goodness knows! We never accepted it, so we kept on forgetting what life was about! I could never accept it in you, nor you in me. I could accept my own life, even that blank misery, that self-perpetuating woe, but I could not abide to see you afflicted, nor could I stand that misery in your eyes when you saw me suffering. Perhaps that's love. I don't know. Perhaps we really did love each other? Now isn't that a strange thought? Anyway. However.

Do you remember the day you drove the nail into your own hand? remember how we both laughed as if it were the funniest thing ever? You clumsy bonehead, you darling! It could only have been you, able to pull off a trick like that. The big man, not to stay locked for ever in your dark room writing your dark books, no, you had to prove you could put a plug on the iron, change a bulb, hang a picture. You came downstairs, down out of your black eyrie and took the picture-hook, the small brass nail, the hammer. I saw a rip in the armpit of your shirt when you reached. You held the nail with your left hand, you tapped with the hammer, the nail refused, how dare it! you tapped again, viciously, the nail slipped and your left hand slipped and the hammer, already moving . . . and there was the nail, driven through the soft flesh between your fingers! To see your face then, you – clown! stunned before the irrationality of the universe.

There was a robin's beakful of blood. Your hand, held by the merest web of flesh to the wall, shivering. I couldn't help it, and I laughed. Laughed and laughed. Your face changed from shock to amazement to resentment and then to amusement and you laughed too, at the ignominy of it. Afterwards we sat together on the couch and laughed ourselves into sexual longing that we had not shared for such a very long time. Oh if only out of affliction we could reap even the heroism of foolishness! There is purity in that kind of pain, honour in that kind of defeat.

There I go, interrupting myself again! However. Anyway. Where was I? I was saying. There comes a moment when you know that choices have all gone. Where there's only one course left. Let me say at once, for the first time in thirty years, let me say it: *Dearest, I love you.* I have always loved you. And I know you loved me. I know you love me still, in spite of what I have done. It is yourself you do not love. And I have never, after those first lovely years, never been able to get through to you. So I write to you now to tell you all of this.

We had another row, one of the many few, as you would say yourself. One of those rows that breaks loose, like a stone coming free on the street. I brought you your supper of grease and fat as usual, puddings, rashers, sausages, and your favourite, fried bread. There you were, at your desk, head down between your hands as if you would shake words out of it down onto the empty, accusing page. Like an empty stage, you used to say, lights up and the audience attendant, and the stage stays empty, silent, bare. Nothing. Nothing. And you took it out on me, as usual.

'Supper, dear!' I chanted into the half-lit gloom.

You lifted your woe-filled head and watched me put the tray down before you.

'Any progress with the book, dear?' I asked, knowing how much you resented the question, with all its implications. Ah yes, we lived a life that waltzed on nails, needing the pricks to keep us alert, needing the fights to keep us close.

'I'll never get it done,' you whimpered, looking for sympathy.

'Maybe you're just too old,' I mocked.

'You're two years older.' You were quickly in.

'Leave it to a younger generation,' I said. 'They're cleverer.'

'Cleverer at drugs and robbing old women.' You said.

You knew that would be too much for me, what with our Niall and what he had done. As if I had the sole responsibility for our children, as if you were entitled to spend all your energy upstairs at your black books, not knowing whether Niall was in or out, or what he was up to. I knew at once you were distraught that night, that you had never yet really said what you needed to say in your books. But you went too far and I responded too quickly.

'At least they don't hide the truth from themselves when they're caught out,' I said. 'They can admit their failure, and go back to living an ordinary life.'

You just looked at me as if I were a blank wall. I clattered your knife and fork down beside you and stomped out of the room, humming. You hated me humming, too, my noise like a nail down a blackboard, you always said. You would have loved to throw the teapot after me.

That was the way we loved each other. I should have cried at that moment, I wanted to, but I could not find that release. I looked at the closed door of your study and I longed to stretch to you, to be young and light-boned again and be taken in your arms and held, fondled, whispered to. Lightsome things. Flurries of snow-blossom words. But how impossible that was. How impossible. Downstairs – there was nothing. The kitchen, the chores, the pointlessness. I turned and went up to bed. I took my tablets and drew down that thick, silencing blind on another day.

Dearest, every moment of every day someone somewhere comes up against something she cannot bear. And every moment, you too, dear, move a little closer to that moment you will not be able to tolerate. So I have been trying to get through to you.

That next morning I was up hours before you. You wake suddenly, after the tablets, as if a door had opened quickly into your life. I could not lie on in bed in the pool of my own silence. I put on my slippers and that stained, light blue quilted dressing gown you hated so very much. I pulled the curtains and let the grey light of another day dribble in from the street outside. Then I took the two tablets, as usual, with a little sip of water. I stopped, realising I had reached a point where I could not face another day, either with that misery, or without it. It was no flash of genius, no bells rang, no floorboards collapsed. It was simply a certainty that there was no longer any choice, that there was only one thing to be done. I stood there, somewhere between the past and the future, unable to face either way, stuck in a present which was unendurable. Between times. There.

Everything was the same and everything was different. I noticed everything. I was close to being just one more object among all the other objects; I observed them as companions, the way the rubber tip hung off my slipper, the way the talc fell to the carpet, whitening it imperceptibly, as our heads had gone white over the years, dearest, the knob on the door, how it had tarnished, the little chips gone from the wood . . . as if I had already entered a new world and was taking note of everything. The decision taken, it was as if everything had been resolved and I went about my tasks with calm, almost pleasurable dignity.

I opened the front door and took in the milk bottles. And every moment sang and hummed about me! Every sound, the tinkle of the bottles, the click of the door-latch, some bird singing in some back garden. Everything. Time had always dragged me along, you see, often in directions I had no desire for, doing me violence, forcing me on. Now that was over, now I was in command. Can you understand that? me standing there, in the hall, at the foot of the stairs, holding two milk bottles up before me, just . . . being! Time's violence could do no more; it had finally shattered the fabric of my days and through the rip in that fabric eternity was flowing in.

I moved into the kitchen. Boiled the kettle. Set the two places at table. As usual, all as usual. I had myself a cup of tea. One slice of toast. Buttered. I rinsed the cup, the plate, left them to drain. As usual. Which puzzled you, later, that I could have gone through with such a routine. You thought it came on me all of a sudden, just an impulse. Otherwise, you thought, I would have left you a note. But you understood, without any note. You understand, but you won't accept the truth. And that is why I have not been able to come through to you, you won't let me in, your suffering has taught you nothing. You have built a wall of self-justification around yourself. Even from here I cannot reach you. I should have left a note. Saying what I'm saying now. But I couldn't put words on it then. Now you won't let me in. And you won't let me go, either. And here I am, waiting.

Anyway and however. I went out into the scullery and made sure the outer door was locked. And the little window. I closed the door into the kitchen. I contemplated putting a towel under the door, but I didn't, I know now that there was still some tiny part of me yearning to call out to you, for help. I turned on the four rings on the gas cooker. I heard the gentle hiss of the gas. I could see nothing. I thought, for a moment, of my mother, and I was three or four years old again, and had cut my knee, and she was there, consoling me, whispering . . .

I stood, leaning back against the kitchen door. My mind quiet. My heart still. I could not smell anything. Then I opened the oven door and turned on the gas in there. My knees hurt against the cement floor of the scullery. I took two towels from the cupboard and spread them on the floor. I knelt down again, my old body stiff and awkward as I knelt. All I could hear was the soft out-breathing of the gas. I felt a little drowsy. I stretched out on the floor, my head to the oven door. Gradually a sweet, slightly sickening smell began to get to me. I remember yawning. Feeling pleasantly sleepy. Feeling a little nauseous. There was a moment when I felt a choking sensation in my throat, a terrifying feeling as if I was being turned inside out, and I almost panicked, I reached for the oven switch. But the moment passed and a delicious sense of ease and lightness took its place. For some reason I thought of a summer meadow filled with white and purple clovers and alight with butter-cups. There were skylarks everywhere, a blue sky, warmth, and stillness. I felt like singing. I closed my eyes.

When you found me, God help you, you went as still as a rock and as white as one of your sheets of paper. You flung open the back door. You turned off the gas. You went out into the yard and you got sick. You retched and gasped and pleaded with the God you hadn't spoken to for years. You rang 999 and tried to drag me out into the yard. I was too heavy. You were too old. You sat down on the floor and you cried. It was a release. I was whispering to you that it was all right, everything was all right. Even though you were touched by the cold sword-blade of eternity I could not get through to you. You began, at once, your little acts of self-justification, your little tricks of the imagination, filling up the wonderful emptiness you had achieved a moment before, with your shibboleths, your lies. You went searching for a note. You noticed the de-tails of my ordinary morning. It was an accident, you said. All the signs... I threw up my hands in disgust and went away. Or tried to... But I'm still here, for you won't let me go.

Here? You know, I'm still not sure. I'm hovering, like some dandelion puffball, between joy and sorrow, between the world I've left and one yet to come. I haven't let go yet, as you can see, because I know I hadn't allowed myself to finish. I, too, had filled up the emptiness with a trick, with the gas, instead of allowing the God to take over. What does another day's suffering, another year's affliction, take from one who is already without joy or hope? It was a nightmare and I never allowed myself to wake from the nightmare. And so I'm still not sure. The nothingness in me is not yet reached. I came close. But I filled up the void with my own remedy. With my death. I opted out. I have to start again, from here. From this shore.

I have been pleading with you for a long time now. I am tired. I am giving up. I am letting go. It is a shore of some kind but I don't know yet whether I've come to ground here, after drifting in, or whether I have to set out across this strange, still ocean. You know me and water! Terrified of it! Always! And you know me and boats! Hated them! Always! Waves and things, the yawing and barrelling! Anyway and however. Love to you, dearest. Perhaps I'll wait. You'll get this letter, anyway, when you come. It'll be here, an explanation, waiting. Then you'll know. You'll find out. You'll find out...

OTHER FICTION TITLES

from

THE BLACKSTAFF PRESS

IN THE NAME
OF THE WOLF
●

JOHN F. DEANE

'Beyond her pale image in the glass there was only darkness. Almost
now, almost, she could see through her body into the darkness
beyond. She put her hands up around her face and pressed herself to
the window, trying to blot out the images from behind her. Out
there, in that blackness, there was freedom, waiting . . . And then
she knew, with sudden clarity that almost made her laugh aloud.
She knew what she must do. It was so simple, why had she not
known it long before, when she was stronger and more prepared?'

Patty O'Higgins is a young woman suffering from lupus, a disease
surrounded by ancient prejudice and fear because of one of
its occasional side effects, a wolf-like distortion of the face.
Mirroring her illness are strange events in her home community
in the west of Ireland – hatred and anger prowl the mountains,
friend turns against friend and everywhere is the sense of an
overpowering malevolence.

Venturing into the no-man's-land that lies between the warring
forces of our existence – good and evil, sickness and health, love and
death – John F. Deane emerges triumphantly with a cautionary
but surpassingly compassionate novel.

'Deane's compassionate painstaking delineation of these rural lives
gives the book its texture. The characters are warm, flawed and
disturbingly familiar.'

FIONA McCANN, *SUNDAY TRIBUNE*

'It is dark and unsettling reading matter, but there are downright
funny moments which serve to make the characters credible and
the outcome even more appalling.'

JO ROGERS, *IRISH POST*

'an intense writer and lyrical'

BOOKS IRELAND

216 x 138 mm; 176 pp; 0–85640–640–6; pb
£8.99

THE HAPPY PIGS

•

LUCY HARKNESS

Policing is a macho world but Louisa Barratt is tough – isn't she?
She joined the police on a personal mission to make London's
streets safer for women and girls by locking up some of the bad
guys – six years later she's on a Child Protection Unit at King's
Cross Station and suffering badly from compassion fatigue. She
needs out, but how can she leave Candy, the rape victim who has
no one else to turn to, or JJ, the perfect (police)man who may
just be falling in love with her?

When Louisa is attacked in the street by a would-be rapist she fights
back savagely, determined not just to be another victim herself.
Next day, her new boss fails to turn up for work . . .

Written by a former police officer, this is a uniquely accurate
portrayal of police life. It is also an outstanding new novel about a
smart, conscientious young woman trying to keep her sanity
and sense of humour in a world gone barking mad.

'Harkness writes from the perspective of one who knows her
field . . . the novel draws a convincing behind-the-scenes portrait of
the policing world . . . well-written and researched'

ROSITA BOLAND, *IRISH TIMES*

'It's a pleasure to read a well-crafted crime novel written by a real
police officer.'

RTÉ GUIDE

198 x 129 mm; 256 pp; 0-85640-656-2; pb
£7.99

THE DANCERS DANCING

•

ÉILÍS NÍ DHUIBHNE

In this richly complex new novel, Éilís Ní Dhuibhne, one of
Ireland's most exciting and original writers, uses the experiences
and emotions of girls on the cusp of womanhood to explore
dangerous territories of sex, politics, class, and Irishness.

'Ní Dhuibhne conjures the agonies and the revelations of teenhood
with wholly original skill. Her observations are lemon-fresh, her
writing beautiful, witty and wry.'

SUNDAY EXPRESS

'Ní Dhuibhne's writing is marvellous, building layers of
impression until a complex, vital and true-false picture of
liberation is revealed.'

KATHY CREMINS, *IRISH TIMES*

'With a delicate touch not unlike Arundhati Roy's in *The God of
Small Things*, Ní Dhuibhne sneaks under the ill-fitting skin of
her metamorphosing Derry and Dublin cast. Their stories
unravel in shifting voices with all the wisdom and perspective
of an omniscient narrator.'

DEIRDRE MULROONEY, *SUNDAY BUSINESS POST*

'Anyone who has ever attended an Irish college in the Gaeltacht
will recognise almost everything in this book ... an absorbing
read, a rites-of-passage story that is more familiar and
intimate than the usual.'

EITHNE TYNAN, *SUNDAY TRIBUNE*

'When is the world going to discover Éilís Ní Dhuibhne?'

DES TRAYNOR, *BOOKS IRELAND*

216 x 138 mm; 248 pp; 0-85640-650-3; pb
£7.99

ORDERING BLACKSTAFF BOOKS

All Blackstaff Press books are available through bookshops. In the
case of difficulty, however, orders can be made directly.
Indicate clearly the title and number of copies required and
send order with your name and address to:

**BLACKSTAFF PRESS LTD
BLACKSTAFF HOUSE
WILDFLOWER WAY
APOLLO ROAD
BELFAST BT12 6TA**

Please enclose a remittance to the value of the cover price plus:
£2.50 for the first book plus 50p per copy for each additional book
ordered to cover postage and packing.
Payment should be made in sterling by UK personal cheque or sterling
draft, made payable to Blackstaff Press Ltd, or by Visa or MasterCard.

Please debit my Visa* MasterCard* account
*Cross out which is inapplicable

My card number is

Signature

Expiry date

Name on card

Address

Daytime telephone number

Applicable only in the UK and Republic of Ireland

For further details please contact 028 90668074 (phone)
028 90668207 (fax) or books@blkstaff.dnet.co.uk (e-mail)